Christmas with the Coxwells

The Coxwells #5

DEBORAH COOKE

ISBN-13: 978-1-989367-21-6

Books by Deborah Cooke

CONTEMPORARY ROMANCE

The Coxwells:
Third Time Lucky
Double Trouble
One More Time
All or Nothing
Christmas with the Coxwells

Flatiron Five:
Simply Irresistible
Addicted to Love
In the Midnight Hour
Some Guys Have All the Luck
Bad Case of Loving You (2019)

Secret Heart Ink
Snowbound
Spring Fever
One Hot Summer Night
Under the Mistletoe (2018)

PARANORMAL ROMANCE

The Dragonfire Novels
Kiss of Fire
Kiss of Fury
Kiss of Fate
Winter Kiss
Harmonia's Kiss
Whisper Kiss
Darkfire Kiss
Flashfire
Ember's Kiss

Kiss of Danger
Kiss of Darkness
Kiss of Destiny
Serpent's Kiss
Firestorm Forever
Here Be Dragons (2018)

The Dragons of Incendium:
Wyvern's Mate
Nero's Dream
Wyvern's Prince
Arista's Legacy
Wyvern's Warrior
Kraw's Secret
Wyvern's Outlaw
Celo's Quest
Wyvern's Angel
Nimue's Gift

The Prometheus Project
Fallen
Guardian
Rebel
Abyss

SHORT WORKS
An Elegy for Melusine
Coven of Mercy

&

For information about Claire Delacroix historical
romances, please visit:

HTTP://DELACROIX.NET

CHAPTER ONE

December 2018

Beverly Coxwell wasn't feeling festive.

It was the twenty-first of December and snow was falling in the small town of Rosemount, just east of Boston, where the Coxwell family home was located. The house, Grey Gables, seemed to get more beautiful with age. Beverly thought the mock-Tudor house was at its best when decorated for the season.

Each year, Beverly was surprised by how talented her daughter-in-law Leslie was with decorations. She'd never expected such creativity from such a serious academic, which just proved that everyone had hidden talents.

She particularly liked that the house looked fabulous and she didn't have to do anything to make it so. There were advantages to living with her son and his wife, and one of them was having the younger couple do a lot of the work.

There was a massive spruce Christmas tree decorated in red and gold in the foyer, with thousands of fairy links winking each night. There was another slightly smaller tree in the formal living room, this one resplendent in green and red, and yet another, smaller again, in the library that her son Matt used as his office.

There was cedar roping strung on the porch outside and along the roof, plus a massive wreath on the front door, eggnog in the fridge and fires crackling on the grate. All of her children were coming to spend Christmas day at the house Beverly had lived in most of her life, and her grandchildren had all promised to make appearances. She knew that wouldn't last much longer. They'd be getting married and dividing their time soon.

Actually, it wouldn't hurt if some of them got married soon. Beverly wasn't getting any younger and great-grandchildren would be wonderful. She was glad that the entire family was healthy and happy. Who would have guessed that they'd find such tranquility after the challenging years that had come before?

There were presents under the tree already and their meal would be wonderful. Enough snow had fallen to make it look festive, but not so much to impede travel: the roads were clear and there was no foul weather in the forecast.

But it wouldn't be like Christmas for Beverly, even so.

She had been stone-cold sober for thirteen years, one month and seven days, and for the first time in a long time, she was itching for a drink. No, she was ready to kill for one. She could almost taste that glass of sherry, and she knew what kind she'd buy. She knew what glass she'd pour it into. She knew how it would collide with her tongue, then send sweet heat right to her toes. She wanted it. She burned for it—even though she knew one glass would slide into another, and she'd finish the bottle before she knew what she was doing—and everything she'd achieved over the past thirteen years would vanish.

She didn't want to start over again.

The thing was that the sherry would bring oblivion, at least for one night, and Beverly wanted a bit of that, immediately if not sooner.

She stared out the window, clutching the drape, hollow with loss. The house echoed with silence: there was no sound of nails on hardwood, no contented sighs from the floor at her feet, no jingle of license tags as the girls sought her out. Leslie had put everything away—the dog beds, the stuffed toys, the balls, the bowls, the leashes—but Beverly thought it was worse not to see them than to be confronted with the evidence of dogs in residence when there weren't dogs in residence.

How could it be Christmas without Champagne to merrily shred wrapping paper as it was discarded?

How could it be Christmas without Caviar waiting patiently for a taste of the roast turkey? How could it be Christmas without the girls racing through the house in excitement, bows on their collars and tinsel in their tails?

It wasn't Christmas. It couldn't be. Beverly would trade it all in a heartbeat for one last snuggle with the standard poodles she hadn't even wanted to bring home that first day. They'd had good long lives, and she knew it, but Beverly wanted more.

The doorbell rang but she only heard that there were no barks of excitement, no sound of two large dogs rushing to greet whoever arrived. Beverly bowed her head, unable to stop her tears.

She blew her nose, recognizing the low tones of Ross's voice. She'd been seeing him ever since she'd inherited the girls and had taken them to the vet, who had proved to be Ross. Though he was younger than Beverly, that troubled her and not him. He'd been persistent, and he was wonderful company. He made her laugh and he made her feel young—and he made love so sweetly that she wondered where he'd been all her life. He'd moved into Grey Gables ten years before and was an easy calming presence in the house. They'd claimed a bedroom for their own, and a second for a study, then renovated a large bathroom, incorporating another small bedroom to make it even larger. It was a private luxury suite and their retreat. Beverly loved it.

And she loved him.

Which was why she'd declined to marry him, twice.

If Ross asked her to marry him again, today, she might just be weak enough to agree.

Ross came to her and she tried to smile, but he was too perceptive to be fooled. "It's a tough time of year for those who have lost someone," he said, and gave her a sweet kiss. His touch and his sympathy made her feel a little less alone.

"Thank God you talk about them as if they were people."

"Poodles think they're people," he said easily. "I'm inclined to agree." He nodded at the window. "Caviar would have loved this snow."

Beverly nodded. "She could never chase enough snowballs." She bit her lip. "I'm glad it snowed on her last day." Even though the dog had been losing her hearing and her sight, Caviar had brightened at the sight of the first flurries in September. They'd gone outside together and Beverly had been glad to see Caviar play in the leaves, not quite as joyously as she had done once, but more than had become typical. When they'd come back inside, Matt had lifted Caviar onto the couch to sleep beside Beverly while Beverly read, and she'd smiled at the little sigh of contentment as the dog went to sleep.

Caviar hadn't awakened again.

It was a kind end and Beverly knew it. Caviar had been looking for Champagne, her sister and playmate, for six months, since Ross had found a tumor and they'd had to put Champagne to sleep.

Beverly had to believe that the two poodle sisters were together, over the Rainbow Bridge, playing in the snow together.

Ross kept his arm around her shoulders. "They were healthy until the end, Beverly. Fifteen years for Champagne, almost sixteen for Caviar. That's impressive."

"It's not enough," she said, not troubling to hide her anger with that.

"It's never enough," he agreed. "I'll never forget the sight of you three in the Jag, top down, the girls' ears blowing in the wind. I think I lost my heart with one look."

"They loved that car." Beverly took a breath. "I'm going to sell it." She felt Ross's surprise.

"Because the girls are gone?"

"Because it's old enough that it needs pampering."

"Kind of like us?" he teased and she smiled.

"I have to keep taking it in for little tweaks. I want something more reliable, so I was thinking of selling it to the young man at the garage. He seems to love it as much as I do."

"How so?"

"He always polishes it for me. Inside and out. It looks wonderful when I pick it up. He said he'd buy it if I ever wanted to sell, and I'm going to talk to him about it after the holidays."

"And then we can go shopping for cars. That'll be fun."

Beverly grimaced. "That'll be a slice of hell. I

don't know why they can't just tell you the price, instead of all these games of negotiating. I hate buying cars. Maybe we'll just use yours."

"The station wagon isn't exactly your style."

"I don't want to have style without the girls." She sounded like a grumpy child and she knew it. But the desire for a sip was raging, fed by her grief.

"You sound more like the Grinch than the spirit of Christmas."

"I want a drink," Beverly said savagely. "I know I shouldn't have one, and I'm trying to be strong, but it is killing me."

"Maybe you need a distraction, then."

She gave him a hostile glance, only to find his own expression more solemn than usual. She felt a stab of guilt then, that she'd been so self-absorbed that she hadn't noticed his mood. "What's wrong?" She noticed that the line of his mouth was grim and she guessed that something terrible had happened—but Ross was too kind to lay his own burdens at her feet when she was hurting.

"I'm not sure you want to know." He sighed and she knew it was bad.

"Tell me. Distract me, if nothing else."

Ross frowned and shoved his hands into his pockets. "We were called to a farm this morning by the police. They'd had an anonymous abuse complaint."

Beverly caught her breath. "What kind of abuse?"

He met her gaze steadily. "Animal abuse."

She sat down, knowing how much these incidents troubled him. "Tell me."

Ross shook his head. "No. I won't." He took a deep breath. "Except to say that there are days when I find it hard to feel a love of humanity."

Beverly tugged his hand so that he sat down beside her. She gave him a hug this time and felt how he needed it. "You have the kindest heart in the world."

"There were puppies, Beverly," he admitted into her neck. He pulled back and held up three fingers.

Beverly's heart stopped. Three puppies. She couldn't ask if they were okay or not because her throat was too tight.

"Eight weeks old or so. Just about ready to be sold, which is probably why they're the healthiest of them all. They were also nursing."

"The mother?"

"She's a sweet girl, but very thin. I guess she got the food because of the puppies, but she's not in good shape. Still, she tried to defend them so her spirit is strong. One of the techs at the practice has taken her home to see if she can improve her condition over the holidays. Maddie is really patient and she's planning a quiet holiday with her husband, so I'm optimistic. If she succeeds, the mother could be looking for a forever home in the new year."

"Those puppies," Beverly whispered.

Ross met her gaze. "They're in a crate in my car. I need someone to take care of them for the holidays. No one should adopt a pet over the holidays, especially a puppy. They need routine and a calm environment, not the chaos of Christmas. They've had enough," he said, his voice hardening. "They just need some kindness before they learn that the world doesn't offer any. They also need to be weaned and could be trained at this point."

"I'm not keeping them," she protested quickly.

"That's not what I'm suggesting," Ross said. "Just ten days of puppies in the kitchen, and in the new year, we'll find them good homes." He squeezed her hand. "They might make you smile. It could be win-win."

Beverly looked away, torn and a little bit frightened. "I don't know anything about puppies. The girls were adults when I got them, trained and everything. I could make it worse for them, because of my inexperience."

"It's not complicated," Ross said with a confidence she didn't share. "They'll play together and sleep together. I'll be here at night to help, too. They don't seem to have any concerns about the crate, so they'll use it as a cave and a haven. When they stand up, take them outside, then tell them how clever they are when they relieve themselves out there."

Beverly smiled at that. "Maybe they aren't very clever."

"Oh, I think they are. That's why I'm so worried about them." He held her gaze. "They're standard poodles, Beverly. Caramel colored like their mom."

She caught her breath. "If I say no?"

"They'll stay at the clinic for the holiday break and my techs and I will go in as often as we can." He frowned. "But the socialization of a house would be better for them. They can still move beyond their experience."

"You live here, too. You could just bring them home."

"But it's not my house. I can't make this decision and impose it on you all."

Even though he wanted to do it.

"Beverly, this situation we have here works because we're considerate of each other. I want everyone to be in agreement if we do this."

Beverly frowned. "But everyone's coming for Christmas Day. Won't that be too much for them?"

"This kitchen is huge," he said, gesturing to that end of the room. "I was thinking we could partition off the section by the door to the yard and put the crate in there. It would be their little domain, and keep them from getting underfoot. People could visit, but they'd have their sanctuary. We can eat at the counter for a few weeks. Matt can help me move the table and chairs somewhere else. And really, we only have the one busy afternoon here." He smiled at her, an appeal in his eyes that she always found hard to resist. She sensed that he needed to do something to erase what he had seen earlier in the day. "I've brought everything we'll need."

"But you have to ask Matt and Leslie, too."

"They'll be agreeable if you are. Everyone knows

how much you miss the girls, Beverly."

"You knew I would agree."

"I really hoped you would."

Beverly took a deep breath. "I decided when you said they were poodles," she admitted and Ross grinned. "Poodles are people, which means they can't spend Christmas in jail."

"The clinic isn't jail!"

"It might as well be. All those crates, the smell of antiseptic. The girls never liked going there, except for seeing you. And they'd be alone at night, which would be hard for them."

"Agreed."

"They'll miss their mom the most at night."

Ross nodded. "We'll try the old trick of an alarm clock wrapped in a towel, but I doubt they'll be fooled."

She shook her head, filled with new purpose. "We can move that rolling kitchen island to block the doorway for now, but I'll ask Philippa to lend us a few baby gates. I'm sure she can bring them over today. And we can get the leashes out from wherever Leslie has put them, and the bowls..."

Ross seized her hand. "Come help me bring them in."

"If I lose my heart to these dogs, it'll be all your fault," she said, trying to sound stern, but Ross only smiled.

"Just for the holidays," he insisted as they walked down the hall to the front door. Matt came out of the library and Beverly asked him about the plan as they both put on their coats and boots.

"Good idea," Matt said with a smile. "The house is too quiet."

"They might howl all night," Ross warned.

"I think we can survive, right Mom?"

Beverly nodded agreement, excited at the prospect of seeing the puppies. Matt came out to the station wagon with them and Beverly gasped when Ross opened the back gate. Three little faces looked up at her, their eyes bright with hope, their tails wagging so hard that two of them fell over.

"Adorable," Matt said with approval. "Boys or girls?"

"All girls," Ross said and opened the crate.

Beverly picked up one puppy, her heart squeezing tightly at the bundle of softness in her hands. It licked her fingers then grazed them with its teeth, still wagging. "Do they have names?"

"Of course not," Ross said. "We put dots on their backs to tell them apart, since they look so similar."

"Red, blue, and green," Matt said, holding a wriggling puppy. "Maybe we can do better than that."

"I wouldn't recommend naming them," Ross said, handing Matt the third puppy, then lifting the crate out of the back of the car. "It'll make them harder to send them on their way in the new year."

"Hello, Honey," Beverly said to the puppy she was holding and heard Ross's snort. Honey had a red dot on her back. She reached out to the puppy with the blue dot. "Hello, Amber."

"Uh oh. We need another yellow food," Matt said.

"No," Beverly was decisive. She patted the puppy with the green dot. "This is Goldilocks."

"We don't have three bears," Ross teased.

She gave him a look. "Don't even think of adding to the menagerie," she said and they all laughed together. Beverly carried Honey to the house, already unable to think about letting the pups go to new homes. It was amazing how quickly they touched her heart. But Ross was right: the arrival of the puppies had already lifted her mood and given her a list of things to do.

These three little furry bundles of joy were even making her feel a teensy bit festive.

JD was parallel-parking the family SUV right in front of his new building when someone honked at him for the second time. This time, the impatient driver held the horn down a long time.

"Almost there," he muttered and pulled the last increment into the spot. He sure wasn't used to driving this huge thing and thought it was better suited to the suburbs than the Seaport. JD put down the window to thank the other driver for his patience—or lack of it—but the brand new gold Mercedes GT convertible roared around him. The windows were tinted too dark for him to see inside, but the driver sure knew his vehicle. The Mercedes turned into the driveway to the parking garage without really slowing down. The driver's window was on the far side and JD saw a silhouette briefly when the arrival opened the garage door. Then the engine revved, the tires squealed and the car slipped beneath the opening door, with only inches to spare. By the time it was open all the way, that guy had probably already parked.

JD shook his head and got out, taking a moment to admire the building. He'd totally lucked out and he knew it. A year of cheap rent in this luxury building was going to be awesome and JD was going to make it count. He was the proud occupant of the smallest unit in this iconic luxury building, perched on Liberty Street with a view of the Atlantic.

He crossed his fingers for the umpteenth time and hoped the senior partner could be convinced to sell the unit to him in a year. If not, maybe he'd hear of another one since he'd be in the building. Even the studio apartment went for close to a million dollars in this building, but then, location was everything.

So were connections.

The spot was tight, leaving only just enough room to open the back gate. JD got the moving cart out with some difficulty, but didn't touch the car parked right behind the SUV. He loaded up the cart quickly in his excitement, locked the SUV, then realized he had no change for the parking meter.

It was the Friday before Christmas. Would he really get a ticket?

The concierge was gone, probably helping another resident. JD chose to be optimistic. He strode to the door, secretly thrilled that his key actually worked, then pushed the cart across the lobby to the elevators. There was a woman waiting there, a gorgeous woman with long dark hair and striking blue eyes. Everything about her was sleek and expensive, from her gleaming hair to her designer purse. Her boots were smooth and tall with spike heels that his stepmother Maralys would have loved. JD took a good look, sure that his opportunities for meeting women had also vastly improved with a change of location. He smiled when she checked him out, but she didn't smile back.

She turned her attention to the elevator instead.

"You'll get a ticket there," she said and he wasn't immediately sure she was talking to him. Her voice was low and sexy, with an accent he couldn't quite identify.

He looked around. "Do you mean me?"

"Of course."

"So, you saw me park."

"I couldn't miss you. It took you long enough. I thought Christmas might come before you were done. Maybe Easter." She spared him a cool glance as he realized she'd been driving the gold Mercedes. "How long ago did you get your license?"

JD bristled. He was a good driver. "It's not my car." He left out the detail about not having a car at all. He'd be taking transit to work and riding his bike, given the rent on this place.

"Well, there's some hope then." She sighed with forbearance and pushed the button again.

"You could have opened the door for me if you saw me parking out front."

She gave him a look. "There's no point in having keyed access if people hold the doors open for just anybody."

Just anybody. Once more, she gave him a sweeping survey and her expression didn't indicate that she approved of what she saw.

"I'm JD," he said, offering his hand. "JD Coxwell."

She gave him a sidelong glance. "Good for you."

"Well, I'm hoping I won't get a ticket this close to Christmas," JD said.

"Hope won't make a difference," she said flatly and pushed the button twice more.

What a princess. JD felt a bit sorry for whoever had to deal with her.

The elevator doors opened in that moment and she stepped into the elevator. JD pushed the moving cart, holding the boxes as the cart bumped over the lip of the elevator. Because he was trying to hurry, the wheels stuck in the gap between the doors.

Of course.

She sighed again, evidently put out that she had to wait on him. "There *is* a service elevator, you know."

"No, I didn't know. Thanks for the tip." JD had

known, but he was only moving a few boxes. When they brought the furniture on Monday, they could use the service elevator.

The queen bee just might have to wait five or ten seconds.

He didn't think it would kill her.

Once he had the cart in the elevator, he realized that she hadn't pushed a button for any floor. She just stood there, tapping her toe with impatience. He glanced at her. "Just here for the ambiance?" he asked, because he thought she deserved a little jab.

She smiled and the sight took his breath away. Then she frowned and he felt her disapproval again. "Can't be too careful in elevators with strangers."

"I'm moving in. I might not be a stranger long."

"Or you might *always* be a stranger." Her expression hinted that would be her choice.

Right. JD pushed the button for his floor.

The doors closed and she didn't push a button. She stood with her arms folded across her chest, that toe tapping. The elevator rose silently and quickly to JD's floor and despite the company, he felt his anticipation rising.

His companion stared at the panel displaying their progress, clearly bored.

He tried to think of something clever to say, but didn't manage it by the time the doors opened. And really, it would have been a wasted effort with her.

He eased the cart into the hallway and would have wished her a nice day at least, but she strode out of the elevator at the last moment and swept past him.

Kind of like that gold Mercedes.

The heels of her boots clicked as she marched to the end of the corridor—where JD guessed there was a large unit that wrapped around the end of the building—and she didn't look back. She did have great legs, and her jeans showed her butt to advantage. JD watched, because he was heterosexual, and because he had a feeling it would piss her off.

She was walking so quickly that he halfway thought she'd collide with the door, but the door was opened just before she reached it. Bright light flowed from the apartment, probably sunlight shining though a lot of big windows, and a guy who must have opened the door was silhouetted for a moment. Did he bow? JD supposed that some people in this building might have staff and that the staff would show deference. *However you like it, madame.* That made him smile.

The way she walked into the apartment without slowing down reminded JD of the way the car had slipped under the opening door to the garage. He found himself looking down the hall at a closed door.

If she lived on the same floor, he might see her again and learn more. That might not be such a good thing. He chose to forget his snobby neighbor. He might have a whole bunch of them, after all.

JD opened the door and grinned at the space. It was a small apartment but, empty, it looked bigger than it was. The hardwood floor gleamed and the large windows shone. The senior partner had ensured that it was cleaned out and it looked massive compared to when JD had seen it with furniture. He pushed the cart over the threshold, locked the door behind himself, then went to check out the view.

It was as awesome as he remembered.

This was it. The start of his new life. He'd finished articling and passed the bar; he had a job in a good firm and the partners liked him. He was on his way, following in his dad's footsteps. Maybe he'd become the fiercest defense lawyer in Boston, just as his dad had been before he moved over to the D.A.'s office. Now James Coxwell was the fiercest prosecution lawyer in Boston. His dad won, and JD aspired to have the same mojo in the courtroom. Maybe JD would become a judge, like his grandfather. The world was out there, waiting for JD and his ambition.

He turned away from the view with reluctance, then unloaded the boxes of kitchen stuff and bathroom stuff before heading back down to the car. He glanced down the hall while he waited for the elevator but he could have been alone in the building.

Two more loads and JD was almost done. The concierge had returned to his post and after checking JD's credentials, held the door open for him each time. He checked his watch and saw that he didn't have a lot of time to get to the airport and pick up his mom. She was flying in from Phoenix for Christmas with her current boyfriend, and borrowing the SUV meant that he got to play chauffeur. He hurried back down to the street and loaded up the cart one last time. This load was heavier, with his stereo, speakers and records. JD was old-school when it came to music and had a serious vinyl collection. He was shutting the gate when a cherry-red Porsche zoomed past him and turned into the driveway for the parking garage, squealing its tires. He was pretty sure it was a 911 and new. It certainly was polished to a high gleam.

"Same driving school," he muttered to himself as this driver paused to unlock the garage door and raced toward it before it had fully opened.

He was coaxing the cart into the elevator when a tall guy with dark hair appeared beside him. He must have come out of the door to the parking garage. The concierge nodded to him in greeting.

"Need a hand?" he asked and took the corner of the cart without waiting for an answer. They got the cart into the elevator together, and the doors closed right away.

JD hit the button for his floor.

"Hey, we're neighbors," the other guy said and offered his hand. "Michael, but most people call me Mike."

"James, but most people call me JD." They shook and JD noticed that Mike had blue eyes. There was more than that about the other man's appearance that reminded JD of the woman. Mike was well-dressed and had the assurance of wealth. He also had a similar accent as the woman, though JD still couldn't place it. Even so, he could guess which apartment Mike lived in. "Are you in the apartment at the end, to the right?"

Mike nodded. "The three-bedroom plus unit." He rolled his eyes. "It's not nearly big enough."

JD grinned. He'd seen the floor plans. "Lots of stuff?"

"My sister Sylvia has enough clothes and shoes to dress everyone in the state." He rolled his eyes. "No good deed goes unpunished, that's for sure."

"How so?"

"I said she could stay for a month or two. That was two years ago. The third bedroom is her closet now."

"A closet with a great view."

Mike laughed. "A wasted view. You have a sister?"

JD nodded. "One. But she's too young to be much trouble."

"Wait for it," Mike said as the doors opened at their floor. "Sylvia's a royal pain." He laughed a little under his breath, and JD assumed it was a private joke because he didn't get it.

Between the two of them, they got the cart into the corridor before the doors closed again.

"Vinyl?" Mike said, running a fingertip along the top box. "Looks like you're a serious collector."

"Everyone needs a hobby."

Mike laughed. "I'll stick with flash cars and

beautiful women."

JD could only wish for hobbies like that. At the moment, he didn't have the cash. He offered his hand again. "Thanks for your help."

"No problem. Welcome to the building."

"Great car, by the way."

Mike grinned. "Thanks. I'll give you a ride sometime." He waved and strode toward the end of the hall, to the same door the woman had entered. Just as with the woman—*Sylvia*—the door was swept open in perfect time for Mike to stride into the apartment without slowing down. Once again, the guy at the door bowed.

But this time, JD thought the guy addressed Mike as "your majesty."

Was he hearing things?

JD didn't have time to think about it. He knew there was going to be traffic on the way to Logan and he was running later than he'd hoped. He unloaded the boxes, took one last look at his new view then went back down to the SUV. The concierge confirmed his plans for moving in, and said he'd arrange for the furniture to be put in the apartment when it was delivered Monday. JD knew he could get used to living like this.

He'd put the cart in the back and was unlocking the door when he saw the ticket tucked beneath his windshield wiper.

Crap.

She'd been right after all.

He glanced up, way up to the tenth floor and

wondered if Sylvia was watching and laughing at him. She was the type who would enjoy the misfortunes of others. Just in case, he plucked the ticket off the windshield then waved cheerfully before heading to the airport.

It wouldn't be all bad to see Sylvia again, despite her attitude, even if just for the eye candy. Who knew? He might wear her down with his charm over time. JD laughed at the very prospect. There wasn't enough charm in the world to wear Sylvia down.

He didn't care. All was good. He had a place of his own in a great building and one year to make his mark. His neighbors could be as miserable as they liked.

A royal pain.
Your majesty.
Were Sylvia and Mike royalty?
If so, from where?

CHAPTER TWO

Anymore or any more?" Annette asked, addressing the question to the world at large. It was already dark outside and the shadows were long inside the industrial loft she shared as a workspace with her cousin Jonathan. Her aunt Maralys had built her software business here, in a building that had once been a pickle factory in downtown Boston, and Jonathan had taken over the space when Maralys sold her business and hung up her keyboard. At night in the winter, it seemed to Annette that the space recalled its roots: the cold that emanated from the old bricks always carried a whiff of vinegar. If it got really cold, she could smell dill. She tugged on a pair of fingerless gloves that she kept nearby and considered the design for a new T-shirt.

"Anymore or anymore?" Jonathan echoed.

"Anymore or any space more," she clarified.

"Depends on context," Jonathan said on his side of the space. They'd divided it with a solid yellow line, like one down the middle of a paved road, with dashes for passing from Annette's side on one half of the line, and dashes for passing from Jonathan's side on the other. His side was filled with computers and bits of hardware, any one of which was probably important. The far wall was covered with monitors, which had prompted him paying the electrical bill. Annette liked how they glowed and she didn't mind her cousin's sound system either.

Their taste in music varied wildly, though.

Her side of the line was cluttered with supplies and inventory for her T-shirt business. The largest horizontal surface had three silkscreen presses. There were shelves of ink, buckets of embellishments and a massive bulletin board jammed with ideas. The glass brick windows let in a suffused light in daytime that Annette liked a lot. At one end of her space was her carefully stacked inventory, and inevitable, a pile of packages ready to be shipped. The courier stopped in daily, providing some eye candy.

The industrial elevator rose in the middle of the space and the new arrival was confronted with the line, then Jonathan's software business to the left and Annette's T-shirt business to the right. Behind the elevator was a bathroom and kitchen, both of which were showing their age. Even though no one was supposed to stay overnight in the unit, which was zoned industrial, Maralys had lived here and Annette now did, too.

"Context?" she asked, looking across the loft.

Predictably, Jonathan had Googled her question. He was her full service dictionary, glossary and fact-checker, far better than Siri or Alexa.

"Any more, with a space, refers to quantity, while anymore..."

"No space."

He nodded. "...refers to time."

"I don't want any space more orders before the holidays," Annette said. "Because I don't feel festive anymore."

"Exactly." The screen flashed and he returned to whatever he'd been doing before. She knew it was code displayed and that was enough.

Her monitor, in contrast, was showing a graphics program. She completed the image—no space—and sent it to the printer. Once she checked the size and composition on a shirt, she'd make a screen and get to work. This was her last design for the year, and its lack of holiday spirit appealed to her.

Her Goth clients would love it, too.

She'd print it on black T-shirts, then do some on red ones, too. No, burgundy. She still had a good stock of those. Silver ink with a bit of red on the black shirts. Black with a bit of gold on the burgundy ones. It would work.

It was quiet in the loft after that, just the sound of Jonathan's keys tapping, which meant he had his earphones on. Annette glanced over to see that he was nodding in time to some beat. As usual, his massive insulated coffee cup was beside him, steam rising from the top. She made herself a cup of herbal tea in her fave raku skull mug and set to work.

She didn't interrupt him until she'd pulled the first shirt, silver ink on black. It would have to dry before she could add the red accents, but it already looked good. She slipped the T-shirt onto a hanger and crossed the loft, being sure to step over the line where it was dotted on her side. Jonathan was her toughest critic, but he really understood her market. Even if he said something that annoyed her, he was invariably right.

The real reason they had the line was so that they didn't surprise each other. Jonathan could see her coming, even from his peripheral vision, when she crossed in the assigned zone. It had only taken one tragic incident with a cup being knocked over, spilling twenty ounces of coffee into at least three keyboards, to lead to the plan.

He turned and lifted off his earphones as she approached. "The new design unveiled," he said, his tone teasing. He was a good-looking guy, if too serious in Annette's opinion—and as the older cousin, she got to have an opinion, in her view. His hair had stayed chestnut brown and wavy, like his dad's, and he had green eyes. His older brother, JD, had dark hair and blue eyes, favoring their mom more. The brothers couldn't be more different: JD had gone to law school and was ambitious and driven. Jonathan had gone to MIT and half the time seemed to be on another planet, dreaming up the future. Annette considered it her responsibility to remind him to eat and sleep.

"I'd give you the first one, if you'd wear it."

Jonathan read the slogan and smiled. "*'The trouble with society is that no one drinks from the skulls of their enemies anymore.'*" He met her gaze. "The cup runneth over."

"It does. What do you think?"

"The graphic has a kind of punk sensibility that fits the quote. What goes on the back?"

"That'll be the second screening. A line of skull chalices, then the website url. Teeny. Here."

"Are you going to color break it?"

"I was planning for some red. This chalice. Maybe the words society, skulls, and enemies."

They debated the merit of the color break for a few minutes, then Jonathan made a suggestion. His tone was so casual that Annette noticed the difference immediately. "Why don't you ask Tina?"

She propped a hand on her hip, although she was secretly glad that he was aware of any other humans in the world. Still, he needed to learn better how to interact with them if he was ever going to have more than one date with a woman. He was such a geek. "So, she can come here to see it and you can just happen to talk to her and finally get around to asking her to come to Rosemount for Christmas dinner."

Jonathan grimaced and reached for his headphones. "Okay, bad idea."

"Late idea," Annette corrected. "It is the twenty-first. Even the most disorganized people know what they're doing on the big day at this point."

"I'm not disorganized."

"No, you're shy."

"I'm not...!"

"Yes, you are. I don't know why. You don't look half bad, you're smart, you have a successful company, you clean up well."

"Thanks a lot."

"And a geek, if not a nerd."

"Don't go crazy building my confidence here."

"Once you warm up to someone, you don't have a problem with conversation."

"There's a small mercy."

"I'm saying you can do it when you want to."

Jonathan grimaced. "I don't meet a lot of people doing what I do."

"Funny, isn't it?" Annette surveyed the loft. "Stuck in an old pickle factory alone with your computers and you don't end up with a busy social life." She leaned closer. "You need to leave this place sometimes."

"I leave every day!"

"To go home and sleep. That's not quite what I mean."

"I go to my clients."

Annette snorted. "Once a year! Everything else you do online. You're like a hermit, locked in his cave, letting his toenails grow to epic proportions..."

"I have better grooming than that."

"Good thing."

He lifted a finger. "And I go to the gym, which you do not."

"Right." Annette silently acknowledged that he was right, but exercise was so boring.

Jonathan folded his arms across his chest and gave her a skeptical look. "And I'm supposed to take dating advice from you? The eternal virgin?"

"I'm not a virgin!"

"How would I be able to tell?"

"You are my cousin," she replied sternly. "You're not supposed to be able to tell. That would be gross."

"I mean that you don't have a fabulous social life either."

"I'm picky," she argued.

Jonathan continued as if she hadn't spoken. "Even though you do leave this place once in a while, it's to make deliveries to shops and stalls."

"Owned by women," Annette acknowledged with a grimace. She leaned against the desk. "It is a sad sad thing when the arrival of the courier each day is the man-candy highlight."

"Especially the guy we have now," Jonathan acknowledged.

Annette sighed at the truth of that.

"There's a whole new year coming up," Jonathan said after a long pause. "And New Year's is a great time for resolutions."

Annette marched back to her side and hung up the shirt to dry. "I hate resolutions. I never keep them, so I end up feeling like a loser."

Jonathan followed her. "So, we police each other."

"What is it about the word *police* that sets my teeth on edge?"

"We help each other. Coach each other."

Annette turned to look at him. "What's the goal?"

"Sex. More sex for both of us, but not with each other." There was a challenging glint in his eyes and he looked a lot more hot than usual.

"We help each other get lucky?"

"No one else is in line to do it."

Annette smiled. "Good point."

"Think about it." Jonathan was trying to persuade her, which Annette found interesting. "You know women."

"Like Tina."

"I know guys. We should be able to pool resources here and get some excellent results."

"But all the guys you know are at the gym."

"And they have discounts this time of year for new members."

Annette winced. "I don't want to exercise. I want someone who loves me just the way I am."

"I think you're kind of cute, even though you being a relative puts you outside of the field of contenders."

"But...fluffy." Was it better if she said it?

"You just need to believe that you're attractive, Annette. Confidence makes a huge difference."

"Flopping around on a yoga mat like a beached whale isn't going to help with that."

"You're curvy. I know guys who are seriously into that."

Annette regarded him with suspicion. "Hot guys?"

Jonathan nodded.

"And I know women who think nerds are hot," she admitted.

"Sounds like a deal that's destined to be." Jonathan offered his hand. "Should we wait for January or start now?"

"I suppose that depends on whether Tina's available or not."

Jonathan grinned. "I guess it does."

"Well, her schedule rules. If you want to see her, you need to be here whenever she can come. I'm seriously asking a favor for her to drop by this close to Christmas."

"Deal," he agreed easily, returning to his side of the loft. He didn't sit down to work, though, just leaned against his desk and sipped his coffee, watching as she made the call.

She was waiting for Tina to answer when Jonathan cleared his throat.

"I suppose you heard that Grandma is selling the Jag."

"What?!" Annette terminated the call as it went to voice mail. "That's my car."

"It's not your car," Jonathan scoffed. "It's *her* car and she told me today that she's going to sell it. She asked if I wanted to buy it, but I don't."

"She never asked me!"

"Everyone knows you can't afford two vehicles and how would you do deliveries in the Jag? Your Kia is more sensible."

"But I love that car. I learned to drive a stick on that car."

"It's not that reliable anymore," Jonathan said then gave her a look. Their gazes met for a minute. "Knock out some great designs and buy a new one."

"Vintage is better."

"Only if you don't have to pay the mechanic's bills. That's what I told Grandma. I think some guy at the garage is interested." He snapped his fingers. "Hey, maybe you should date him and live vicariously."

"Very funny," Annette said, her mood soured by the news. She called Tina again and waited for the voice mail. She listened to the message, aware that Jonathan was waiting and smiled as she ended the call. "We're off to a lousy start," she told him. "Tina's gone skiing in Quebec for two weeks."

"But you asked and I appreciate it. Now I owe you one."

"Are you going to tell me more?"

"Nope. Just come to the gym with me by New Year's and sign up."

Annette made a face at the prospect of working

out regularly, even of going to the gym.

"Lots of hot guys there," Jonathan said, obviously guessing the direction of her thoughts.

"But do they think about anything other than sculpting their abs?"

"Sex. They think about sex."

Annette admitted that had promise.

"I go there and I don't think about my abs," Jonathan continued.

"Okay." Annette nodded. "Okay. Let's do this thing. I'll go tomorrow and sign up." She gave her cousin the eye. "If I don't get lucky in thirty days, though, I'm going to cancel the membership and the deal."

"Thirty days," Jonathan agreed. "But you at least have to talk to each guy I introduce to you."

"Right. You, too. And we each need go out for coffee, at least, with one out of three."

"Okay."

They met at the line and shook on it. Despite herself and despite the conditions of the deal, Annette found herself looking forward to the new year.

If not the gym.

"Let's consider it a warning," Dr. Wendy Moss said as she stepped back and smiled at James.

James Coxwell didn't smile in return. "A warning of dire things to come," he said, sounding as grim as Maralys felt.

Maralys kept her arms wrapped tightly around

herself, feeling as if she had to physically keep from falling to pieces. It shook her to see James anything less than his usual confident and strong self.

She was used to thinking of him as a kind of Superman, leaping tall buildings in a single bound, solving every crisis, and doing it all calmly and consistently. He wasn't supposed to have a heart attack.

They were in the cardiac section of the emergency ward, far too early on Saturday morning. It was still dark outside, although it was busy enough in the hospital. Maralys knew that she was less than her usual stylish self—something about her husband awakening just after midnight with a moan that sounded ripped loose of his soul tended to mess with her game like that. Later, she'd probably be glad there were no mirrors in the ER. For the moment, she was worried about James.

He looked like hell. Well, slightly better than hell, which she supposed was an improvement. He wasn't as pale as he had been. The man who never got sick, her anchor and her rock, had scared the life out of her just hours before.

"Can we go yet?" James asked, more irritable than was his habit. He picked at the adhesive circle holding a sensor in place on his chest.

"At least you're well enough to be cranky," Maralys said, hoping for a smile.

She got an intent look, which was almost as good. James still looked haggard and those electrodes were stuck all over his chest and back.

The monitor was showing a steady pulse though and whatever the various squiggles meant in that line, Dr. Moss was happier about them now.

The doctor pushed the adhesive back, then lifted her clipboard. "So, let's just do a quick review here. You run five miles three to four times a week."

"Yes, with Maralys."

"You don't need to provide witnesses, counselor," Dr. Moss teased and the corner of James' mouth finally lifted. "This isn't a cross examination."

"Force of habit."

"Your cholesterol isn't bad. You must eat well."

"Maralys took away the red meat," James said. "We have steak twice a month, no more and no less."

"First world problems," Maralys interjected.

"More than a lot of other people," Dr. Moss agreed.

"Point taken."

"Fried foods?"

"Not in my kitchen," Maralys said. "What they eat when they're out is their business."

"I avoid them, on advice of my partner," James said mildly. "But sometimes at lunch, a burger is quick and easy."

"Desserts and sweets?"

James shook his head.

His color was improving by the minute, to Maralys' relief, and she released the breath she hadn't realized she'd been holding.

Then she thought her knees might give out.

The ever-perceptive Dr. Moss caught her elbow. "Easy there. Take a seat, Maralys. He's going to be fine."

"Not if he ever does that to me again," she said and did as instructed.

"You're essentially in good shape, James, despite last night's scare. The cardiologist will come by and see you again this morning, and probably book you in for some tests to be sure we know what's happening. As your GP, though, I'm going to guess that your comparatively good habits have kept this at bay for this long."

"Why doesn't that sound like good news?" James asked.

"Celery sticks forever," Maralys interjected and he rolled his eyes.

Dr. Moss closed her clipboard and looked James in the eye. "It's got to be stress."

"Stress? From having a job? Don't tell me to work any less. We're overloaded at the D.A.'s office already and I can't work fewer hours than my staff..."

"Stress," Dr. Moss interjected, her gaze on the monitor. Sure enough, James' pulse had increased.

"Couldn't possibly be me," Maralys offered and James snorted. "Can't be financial worries either, not now that the boys are finished college. We've got disposable income coming out the wazoo."

"I'm sure you and Zoë will step up." James was giving her a hard time, which was another sign of progress and Maralys was encouraged.

"Not if we need to cut back." She couldn't hold his gaze this time because the prospect of losing him anytime in the next forty years frightened her.

James probably saw, though. He took a deep breath and exhaled slowly, as if preparing to accept the awful truth. "Please don't tell me to start doing yoga."

Maralys smiled a little. It was a joke between them that yoga was his worst fear.

"It wouldn't hurt," Dr. Moss said. "But what I really want you to think about is retiring."

James looked completely stunned. "You mean, stop working?"

"That's what retirement generally means."

"But going to court is all I know how to do." He was exasperated and Dr. Moss pointed to the monitor with her pen.

"And you live on coffee when you're trying a case," Maralys said. "You don't sleep enough those nights, because you're prepping your arguments all the time. You pace like a caged tiger."

"I'm not that bad."

"You're that focused."

"That's how I win!" His eyes flashed. "What am I going to do if I don't do what I do?"

"Get a hobby."

"I am not going to play golf," James said and ripped one of the electrodes free. He winced, but reached for another. "Let's go home, Maralys."

"Work-related," Dr. Moss continued. "I said this

was a warning call, James. In my opinion, if you keep on the way you're going, you'll be back here in a year, or maybe two, and the view won't be so pretty."

James frowned and stopped removing the second adhesive patch. "That bad?"

"If you're lucky," Dr. Moss added. "You might just drop somewhere sometime and leave Maralys with an even bigger mess to deal with than she had tonight."

James glanced at Maralys and she held his gaze steadily, letting him see her fear this time. "You have to be at Zoë's graduation," she said tightly, referring to their thirteen-year-old daughter. "She's going to be valedictorian. I just know it and it'll be because of your influence."

James pushed a hand through his hair. "Retire? I'm only fifty-eight."

"You won't see sixty-five unless you do retire." Dr. Moss smiled. "The cardiologist might sugar-coat it a bit more, but Maralys and I go back long enough to understand each other." She smiled at Maralys. "You do have a tendency to have stubborn men in your life."

James snorted again.

"Thank you for your honest assessment," Maralys said, knowing that this doctor's willingness to speak bluntly had also extended her father's life by several years. She stood up and faced James, knowing that he'd already gone through a dozen possible scenarios and discarded most of them. "We could buy a house in Rosemount, like we've been saying."

"We were going to do that after Zoë finished college."

"We could do it now. Sell the house in Boston. That'll take care of the financing. We'll probably end up with no mortgage and change left over."

"But Zoë won't want to change schools..."

"She just might. She's been a bit lost since Lindsay moved to Colorado." Maralys glanced at Dr. Moss. "Her best friend."

"Ah." The doctor pretended to be engrossed in her charts, but Maralys knew she was listening.

"She might do better in a smaller school, where it's less intimidating to join other groups," Maralys suggested.

"You don't know that it will be."

"And you don't know that it won't be. I say we ask her."

He fixed a hot look on her. "You will not tell her that I'm going to die if she wants to stay in this school."

"No, but you're going to have to tell her something. She did see the ambulance last night and she's not stupid."

James nodded and swung his legs around the bed, as if he'd get up. "All right. We can drive out early for Christmas, look at some real estate, and talk about options. Matt and Leslie probably wouldn't mind."

"You're not convinced," Maralys said.

"No, I'm not, but we can explore the possibilities..."

"You're not going anywhere yet," Dr. Moss said. "Sit back, James. You're waiting on the cardiologist before you check out of this hotel." She smiled at both of them. "Maybe you should take this opportunity to talk about it."

Maralys thanked the doctor again and then they were left alone in the curtained alcove. She folded her arms across her chest again and held his gaze. "If you don't listen to her, I'll kill you with my bare hands," she said with quiet heat. "I never want to do that again."

"We're in perfect agreement there." He beckoned to her, offering the crooked smile that still made her heart somersault. "Come here. I need to hold you while we talk about this."

Maralys was only too glad to comply. She closed her eyes as he wrapped his arms around her and she leaned against his chest, listening to the beat of his heart.

"Rosemount," he said. "I never thought I'd go back there."

"What do you mean? We've talked about buying a place there for years."

"That was just talk. Do you really want to live in a small town?"

"Why not? Something different."

"It is different. I lived there for eighteen years."

"Well, eighteen more, in Rosemount or wherever, would be fine by me."

"Maralys. I'm okay."

"I know." The first tear slid free, loosed now that the crisis was past, and James eased it away with his thumb. He didn't comment on it, just held her close. "You scared me shitless," she whispered.

"Well, that makes two of us," he replied softly and the uncertainty in his voice caught at her heart. "I thought we were doing everything right."

"Sounds like we need to tweak our plan."

"Sounds like it," he admitted and she felt him press a kiss to her temple. "I don't think your nightgown matches your sweatpants or your winter coat, by the way."

"Picky picky. Now you're a fashion critic. I thought I did quite well in the dark, while trying to give you CPR."

"You were great." His arms tightened around her. She felt him take a deep breath. "The way I see it, I've got to nail this change so there's no risk of anyone seeing you at less than your best."

Maralys smiled against his chest. "If that works for you, it works for me."

"Come here and kiss me, Maralys," he murmured in a low growl. "Reassure me that we'll get through this just fine."

"Of course we will..."

"You're the one who finds strength in adversity. Share a bit of that with me this morning."

Maralys sat up and looked into his eyes, raising one hand to his cheek. "I'll share it with you every day and every night for the rest of our lives."

"Let's make that a long time."

"Let's," she agreed, her voice husky, then leaned into his kiss.

There were worse things than turning their lives upside down or moving, and the most terrifying possibility was living without James. Maralys would do whatever was necessary to make sure that didn't happen anytime soon.

Next stop: Rosemount.

CHAPTER THREE

It was Saturday morning when Leslie considered the whiteboard in her office. She was tired, having been awake half the night listening to three adorable puppies cry in the kitchen as if their souls were being torn away. She wasn't sure if the menu for Christmas Day seemed more complicated because of her exhaustion or because it truly was complicated.

She'd wiped the lesson plans and grading from the board, and started with a new chart for the menu. She liked to see everything lined up neatly, and the whiteboard was her favorite tool.

There would be plenty of food on Christmas Day, but the question was whether everyone would be able to have a balanced meal, given their dietary considerations. Leslie had been worried about it for weeks. Now that she was off for the holidays, papers had been marked, and grades had been submitted, she could give the question her undivided attention. She still had a couple of days to make additions.

The first column was for the Omnivores, which were mostly the guys. James, Matt, JD, and herself. The turkey with the trimmings and gravy went in this column, along with roasted squash, green salad, and cranberry. The ham belonged here, too. The desserts—Maralys' trifle, her own apple pie with ice cream, plus a lot of homemade cookies—joined that list, too.

Next column was Gluten-Free: since Nick had found out he was celiac, he and Phil and their kids, Michael, Krista and Alex, had eaten the same foods. Leslie suspected that the kids might deviate from their usual diet, given the choice. They could eat the turkey, and Phil was bringing a gluten-free stuffing that she'd found on Jamie Oliver's website. Zach was making a beet salad to bring as a vegetarian option, but that would work for gluten-free, as well. For dessert, hmm. She'd set out a bowl of mandarin oranges. Nick wasn't much for dessert usually, and the others might indulge.

The third column was Vegetarian, mostly for Jen, although Zach would eat those dishes as well, as would their girls Nicole and Jasinda. Leslie added the three of them to the Omnivore column, because she knew they'd eat turkey. She added Annette and Zoë to both the vegetarian and the omnivore column, knowing how her daughter and niece would mix it up. Jen was bringing a nut roast, and Leslie had added a bean salad in addition to their usual green salad. Plus there would be Zach's salad. Was that enough? Fortunately Jen ate dairy and eggs, so all of the desserts would be okay for her.

Keto was the fourth column. Beverly and Ross were following a low carb diet, as was James' son Jonathan. They wouldn't eat the potatoes or the regular stuffing. Leslie added a lentil side dish that she often made and which was popular. And she'd ask Maralys to bring that side with the roasted brussel sprouts. Beverly had already bought a keto-cheesecake, which was in the freezer. Leslie added dark chocolates to the list of desserts and a fruit salad with a lot of berries. Ross could pick some whole wheat and gluten-free buns from the specialty bakery on his way home from the clinic on the twenty-fourth.

When in doubt, offer bread. That had been her mother's solution and it still worked. She added a cheese tray and olives. Everyone could eat olives. Maybe.

Then Leslie stood back and considered the logistics of it all. The kitchen had a double-oven with eight burners, plus they had the microwave. Was it enough? Half of the space in the kitchen, the area with the table, had been surrendered to the puppies. They might need to retrieve the table as a work surface for staging the meal. The turkey, of course, would claim one oven for most of the day. The ham could be cooked earlier, then the second oven used for the gratin…she jumped when Matt cleared his throat from the doorway.

"It's like a military campaign," he said. "Should we sketch out the strategy on another board?"

"Very funny," she replied. "You like your story boards well enough."

"Can't live without them."

"What do you think? Are all the variables covered so everyone has a good meal?"

"If they don't, they can deal with it once a year." He came into her office and paused beside her, considering. "How does it work with the ovens?"

"That's what I'm figuring out now."

"Do you want me to set the table?"

"Would you? You have a better sense of where everyone should sit."

"Good dishes?"

"Of course! It's Christmas."

He didn't laugh, even though she expected him to, and she turned to look at him, remembering that she'd heard the phone ring. "What's wrong?"

"James had a minor heart attack last night."

"You're kidding. Is he all right?"

Matt nodded and perched on the edge of her desk. "The doctor says it's a warning that he has too much stress from work."

"That's easy to believe. James is pretty driven."

"So, he's already decided to retire, like the doctor suggested."

Leslie blinked. "That was fast."

"You know James and Maralys." Matt smiled a

little. "They're like greased lightning once they assess the variables and make their decision. They want to come out with Zoë tomorrow afternoon to stay while they look at real estate in town. Marcia will come out with the boys on Christmas Day as planned."

"They're going to move to Rosemount? Seriously?"

"Seriously. What do you think?"

"If they want to come and stay early, that's fine by me. The bedroom they always use is already made up since they'd planned to stay Christmas night."

"I thought so, but I told Maralys I'd call back."

She watched him for a minute. "Do you mind the idea of them moving here?"

"No, actually," Matt admitted. "I mean, we grew up here, but we did our own things then. James is easier to talk to now, or maybe I am. Either way, I think it would be good."

Leslie smiled. "Good. Then I think so, too." She pretended to shudder. "Although I can't imagine what Maralys will reorganize once they're here."

Matt laughed. "She can be a force of nature. I think her attention is going to be on James' rehab for the moment, and getting Zoë settled in a new school."

"Do you think JD and Jonathan will move here, too?"

"No. JD just rented a place downtown and Jonathan will probably stay at the warehouse, at least during the week. James and Maralys will be downsizing, I'll guess."

"Did you warn them about the puppies?"

"They quieted down eventually last night."

"About three."

"Well, maybe tonight it will be earlier. They're quiet now."

"Because they didn't sleep last night." Leslie laughed. "They're probably crashed out!"

"No, Mom has taken them out for a walk in the snow."

"They're good for her, aren't they?"

Matt nodded. "She's less sad about the girls. I wouldn't be surprised if she decides to keep one of them."

"I wouldn't be surprised if that was Ross' diabolical plan." They smiled at each other. "Those poor little puppies. I hope Ross finds good homes for them all in January." Leslie went to sit beside Matt, and he took her hand in his. She guessed that he was shaken by his big brother having such an incident. "Are James and Maralys going to be okay, if he retires early?"

"I don't think they'll kill each other," Matt said, his tone teasing.

"No, I mean financially."

Matt shrugged but looked thoughtful. "James wouldn't have been so easily persuaded otherwise. He's very practical." He smiled. "But it makes me feel even better about being able to pay off the last of the loan from the three of them this year."

Leslie's heart clenched. She was so proud of Matt's success yet he was modest about it. That he had earned enough from his books to buy out his siblings so they could own Grey Gables outright just amazed her. "Maybe you shouldn't wait until Christmas to give James his check."

"That's what I was thinking."

"It might make a difference to their housing plans." Matt nodded and she squeezed his hand. "He'll be fine, I'm sure. Maralys won't put up with anything less."

"That's true enough." They shared a smile that heated Leslie to her toes. "Makes you think, though. I'm feeling grateful for all the good things in our lives. For example, I'm glad you have such a long break over the holidays."

"And I'm glad you're taking one from writing. I feel as if we can enjoy the season more this year."

"Well, I just had to get that book done. By the way, Maralys wants us to use their tickets to Handel's *Messiah* tonight. Want to go on a date night?"

"Is this the production in the church that we miss every year?"

"The very one."

"That will be wonderful. And you can give James the check when we pick up the tickets."

"My plan exactly," Matt agreed. "We'll go to the North End for dinner. I already made a reservation." Then he reached up and erased James from the Omnivore column, moving him over to

Keto. "I'll stock up on non-alcoholic options."

"I guess we shouldn't give him that bottle of Scotch now."

"We'll just have to drink it."

"I never believed we'd be free of debt and living in this house, never mind that we'd do it before retirement."

"Me, neither," Matt agreed and gave her a smile that warmed her to her toes. "I'm so glad you encouraged me to publish my first book."

She smiled back at him. "And I'm glad you encouraged me to take a chance on that new college."

Matt sobered and glanced toward the door. He dropped his voice to a conspiratorial whisper, one that made Leslie shiver. "You know, this might be the last time we have the house to ourselves before New Year's Day."

Leslie smiled, knowing exactly what he was thinking—and in perfect agreement. "I've been meaning to ask your opinion about some new lingerie."

"Really?" Matt's eyes lit. "That sounds very intriguing."

"Just the way to spend a Saturday morning?"

"My thoughts exactly," he whispered and stole a kiss.

It felt so good that Leslie stole one back.

And then she lost track of who was stealing what and when.

"A million dollars," Phil said and folded her arms across her chest. She was standing in the kitchen, wondering when she'd become all-mom all-the-time. She knew she'd suggested it, but the reality had been sobering. She'd had this delusion that she could mom half-time or so, then take a class or learn something new herself.

The truth was that she was run ragged.

She'd started the change and wasn't sleeping, which didn't help.

And Nick and the kids were obviously so happy that she didn't want to rain on everyone's parade.

So far on this Saturday, she'd taken Michael to his piano lesson and Krista to her tai kwon do class, Alex was going to a friend's for a Christmas party and sleepover in the afternoon—for which Phil should have made cookies, but she'd stop at the store on the way instead, which meant they were already late—and she still had to finish the Christmas shopping, ideally today.

The thing that had struck Phil when she walked through the door was that every surface in the kitchen seemed to be covered with dirty dishes. The washing machine beeped that it had finished a load as if to greet her, the dryer chimed that it was done, too, which meant that clothes needed to be folded, hung and put away. The fridge was virtually empty, she had no idea what was for dinner, and she'd barely slept the night before thanks to her hot flashes. The cats were circling their bowls, she hadn't even started to prepare the house for

Christmas, and Nick–the eternal enthusiast–wanted to buy a farm.

Today.

In addition to his grandmother's house. Not instead.

In New Hampshire.

Far, far from every human resource.

Phil sat down hard and dropped her purse on the bench by the door, defeated by what she could only see as the prospect of more work.

And less time.

What would she do for a spa day? All alone? With the confidence that everything else was being managed——not that it was just waiting for her return.

A spa week sounded even better.

"That's only because the house isn't habitable," Nick said cheerfully, spreading his maps and charts across the kitchen table. "Well, except for squirrels and raccoons. The land is amazing, though. Really fertile and exactly what we need to expand the heritage seed bank. We could cultivate the seeds in the collection, in rotation, and build up our inventory..."

"We do that here already."

"But Phil, we don't have enough land. We need a farm. We need equipment. We need to dream big. Since you sold out your landscaping business, I thought we could expand. I think we could start selling heritage seeds, do some garden shows, produce a catalog——but we'll need more seed and more land."

Phil cleared her throat.

Nick looked up, surprised to silence.

She gestured to the kitchen and the greater house. "Don't even dare to suggest that I need something more to do."

He obviously heard the frustration in her voice because he folded up the map and came to her side. "You said you want to do it all. I thought you enjoyed it."

"I did think so," Phil admitted, then took a breath. "I was wrong."

He sat down beside her. One thing about Nick that Phil appreciated was that he listened, once she got his attention. "Why?"

"It's too much. I have no time for myself."

Nick nodded. "Okay. Let's hire Pauline again. I never thought we should have gotten rid of her but you were having a domestic moment."

"I was having a budget moment." Phil frowned. "How can we afford her?"

"Cleaning ladies aren't that expensive." He gave her a nudge and she knew he'd try to make her smile. "If you wanted a Lear jet, that would be another thing."

Phil couldn't smile. "But you want a farm." She sighed. "A million dollars."

Nick's eyes narrowed. "Are you worried about money?"

"Aren't you?"

"No. I didn't think I needed to be."

"Maybe we need to review that." Phil didn't mention that it was a good thing Lucia had passed away. She knew that Nick had adored his grandmother, but once a diva, always a diva. Lucia had become even more demanding and capricious in her winter years, especially after her Chief O'Neill had died of a coronary. She'd been lonely and Phil was relieved that she was at rest. The house, it had turned out, had been carrying more mortgages than they'd expected and money had been a bit tight, even though Nick had inherited the house. She supposed he'd inherited the debt, too.

Phil rubbed her brow, feeling overwhelmed by it all.

He watched her with understanding. "Did you sleep much last night?"

"No. Miserable hot flashes." Phil winced, feeling another one coming.

"You're getting all sparkly," Nick said.

"That's one word for it." The heat rolled through her like a tidal wave, or maybe more like a flow of molten lava. She tasted sweat on her upper lip and couldn't shed her coat fast enough. "I want to be naked. In the snow."

"That sounds interesting. Can I tag along?"

Phil laughed despite herself.

"Give me your coat." He hung it up for her as she endured the hot flash, then brought her a glass of cold water. While she drank, he surveyed the kitchen. "I'm sorry that I don't think about the house details. Do you want to look for a full-time housekeeper instead of just a cleaning lady? I like cooking, and Michael will be driving next year, which will help with getting the girls where they want to be. We can get someone to do a lot of the other stuff."

Phil took a deep breath. "I'm not making any money anymore, Nick," she explained with a patience she didn't feel. "The money from the sale of my business and yours is almost all gone in keeping up this house and daily expenses."

He met her gaze steadily. "You didn't tell me."

She smiled a little. "You were planting seeds to save the planet."

"Phil!"

"I thought it might turn around." She sighed. "Actually, I thought that once Lucia died, there would be a bit of money to lighten the load."

"But she'd leveraged every nickel," he said.

"And then some," Phil agreed.

He nodded, sitting down again. "How tight *are* things?"

Phil was glad he asked. She already felt less burdened, and knew that she and Nick would work out a solution together. She wished she'd talked to him sooner. She got her laptop and pulled up all the files while Nick checked on Alex's packing for the sleepover.

That he was whistling when he jumped down the stairs made her smile.

"That's better," he said and gave her a kiss.

"I want some of that optimism of yours."

"It's yours for the taking, Phil, just like everything else." He sat down beside her. "Now show me."

Phil walked through all of their finances with Nick, answering his questions along the way.

"I thought everything was fixed when we sold the theater downtown," he said finally.

"We got rid of as much debt as asset in that transaction. We're saving the interest on the loan at least."

"You should have told me," Nick said, sitting back as he considered what she'd shown him.

"You're the dreamer. I'm the pragmatist."

"But you must have been worried."

"I was. I am." Phil rubbed her temples, hating what she had to say. She knew he had a strong sentimental attachment to the house, but it was like a sea anchor. "But I didn't think you'd like the obvious solution."

He met her gaze steadily. "Let's sell this place."

Phil blinked, astonished that he suggested it first. "Then you'll have no land for planting seeds."

"Not necessarily. We could move into a smaller house." He grinned. "I mean, we don't actually *need* a nineteenth century mansion."

"I thought you wanted it."

Nick shook his head. "I like it, but my memories will always be mine. Mostly, I wanted to stay for Lucia. She would have hated to live anywhere else." He heaved a sigh. "Now that she's gone though, all options are open. The house is a ton of work, and I never loved its quirks as much as she did."

Phil felt lighter already, just knowing they were in agreement. She smiled and he kissed her. "That's better."

"I should have told you sooner," she admitted. "I thought this was going to be a hard conversation."

Nick shook his head. "We have to find the right solution for us, and that means both of us need to be happy. I know you care about the heritage seeds. I thought you'd like the idea of making it more of a business than a registry."

"I do! I'm just tired."

"Fair enough. Let's fix that first."

"And I'm stressed about money."

"That's already getting fixed. We can have an auction for all of Lucia's collections and advertise it online."

"Then the house."

"Then the house."

Phil considered the possibilities. "What if we move to a farm?"

"Out of town? Do you think it would be hard for the kids socially?"

"Maybe. Maybe not. They will probably be moving out in five or ten years."

"Don't count on that with the price of real estate in greater Boston," Nick teased. "Do you want to live in the country?"

"I don't know. I never have."

"Me neither. I think we should give it a try

before committing. And we might have a harder time getting a cleaning woman in a rural area than if we had a small house here in town."

"Plus we know people here."

Nick tapped his fingers on the table. "What if we stayed in Rosemount, but bought something smaller and newer, then looked for farmland that didn't have a house? We might even be able to rent fields if we find an area we like." He took a sheet of paper and started to make a list. The sight of his action plan reassured Phil enormously.

This was going to get fixed. Soon.

"Have I told you recently that I love you?" she said and Nick grinned at her.

"Yes, but you can tell me again anytime you want." He leaned closer and gave her a long slow kiss. "The kids are gone. The house is ours. Why don't I show you how much I love you?"

"Deal," Phil said and kissed him back.

It might have been right before Christmas, but James Coxwell was on a mission. He'd had a scare but he was going to take a lesson from it. He was determined to look at every house available for sale in greater Rosemount and choose one. He remembered Dinah Dishman from high school and was glad that she knew the town as well as she did. There had to be a reason she was the most successful real estate agent in town.

She looked good, trim and professional in her Chanel jacket and dark trousers. Her snow boots seemed a bit incongruous, but he supposed they were practical. Maralys had suggested they wear shoes they could remove easily and Dinah's boots had no laces either. She shoved a chunk of streaked hair behind her ear, her intensity reminding him of a much younger Dinah.

"It's not as promising as it looks," she told him and Maralys when they met in her informal office on the morning of the twenty-fourth. She had commandeered the corner table in the diner on Main Street, just down the block from Jen's knitting store. "There are seven properties, but we can dismiss half of them right away."

"Really?" Maralys said, smiling as the waitress brought her a cup of coffee.

James declined the coffee. "Why?" he asked Dinah.

She angled her laptop so he could see the display. "This one is a convenience store on the highway with living accommodations behind. It's being sold as a business."

"No," Maralys said.

"Exactly," Dinah agreed. "This one is a small apartment building."

"Aren't the commercial listings separate?" James asked.

"Not when the owner lives in, and that's often what happens here. We don't have many landlords with numerous properties." Dinah scrolled down. "This third one is in a crappy part of town."

"Is Rosemount big enough to have a wrong-side-of-the-tracks?" Maralys asked.

"Yes," Dinah and James said in unison, then smiled at each other.

"A townhouse," Dinah continued, then raised her gaze.

"No," James said.

"More than half dismissed then," she said. "But then, it's a time of year when there aren't many listings. There will be more in February."

"I'd like to look now," James said.

"And prices will probably be better in April," Dinah advised. "Because there will be more properties available."

"That's not really a concern. We have a house in Boston to sell, and just want what works for us."

"Which is?"

Maralys presented a list. "A bungalow would be best for us and we'd rather have a newer house than an older one."

"So the two-story Colonial is out," Dinah said. "Nice house, though. Classic."

"We need three bedrooms, at a minimum, and would like an additional room that can be used as an office," Maralys continued.

"Can it be in the basement?"

James and Maralys exchanged a glance. "A dry basement with a high ceiling," James stipulated.

"What if it's unfinished?" Dinah asked. "Would you finish it out yourself?"

James and Maralys eyed each other again. She shrugged. "I don't see why not," James said.

"Might give you a goal," Maralys said with a twinkle in her eye. "Project manager, coordinating the worker guys so the work is done on time and on budget."

James smiled, just a little. He knew that Maralys was worried about him, but he didn't plan on dying anytime soon. He also wasn't going to take on a lot of stress by moving, if he could help it.

Yoga. That was what he needed to do. Find his zen. He took a deep breath, hoping he wouldn't be bored out of his mind after he retired. "So, what do you have?" he asked Dinah.

"One bungalow, new construction, only two bedrooms but an unfinished basement with a bathroom roughed in. You can choose the finishes, and it will be ready April first."

James nodded while Maralys looked at the pictures. "Marble kitchen counters," she said. "And stainless appliances."

"It's an upmarket builder, but a smaller house than you were describing as ideal." Dinah shared the location, which James knew bordered a good neighborhood.

"Is that where Campbell's farm is?" he asked

"Used to be. It's becoming houses now."

"Not a bad location," he told Maralys. "But it's not right in town, if you want to walk places."

She nodded and turned to Dinah. "What else?"

"There's a huge bungalow from the seventies that was custom-built with a view of the sea," Dinah said.

"Whoa!" Maralys said when she saw the price.

"It's a big lot and already landscaped. Four bedrooms and an office, four bathrooms. The house has been for sale for a while and it has its idiosyncrasies." Dinah was scrolling through pictures and Maralys was watching.

"That wallpaper has to go," she said. "I didn't even know they made mint green bathroom fixtures."

"Oh, this house will astonish you in so many ways," Dinah said with a smile. "But it's big, it's on a great lot in an excellent location, and the construction is solid. It's an estate sale and they might welcome an offer just to have it sold."

"So, that's two," James said. "Can we see them today?"

Dinah nodded and pulled out her cellphone.

"What about the Colonial?" Maralys said. "Just for comparison."

"Sure," Dinah agreed. "It's really a nice house, in my opinion, but it's your opinion that matters. Four bedrooms upstairs, an office or fifth bedroom on the main floor, a smaller lot, closer to downtown, separate garage. Nice garden."

"It's pretty," Maralys said as she flicked through the pictures.

It, too, was more expensive than James had expected houses in Rosemount to be. He was really glad that Matt had paid out the last of the family loan made to him to buy Grey Gables. That extra bit of cash would make all the difference.

"Three houses, then," James said in conclusion. "If we could see them all today, that would be great."

Dinah paused. "There's one more you might want to ask about tomorrow."

"Excuse me?" James asked, not understanding.

"I hear a rumor that your sister and her husband might be planning to sell Lucia Sullivan's house. You can probably find out the truth at Christmas dinner." She gave him an impish smile. "Try to remember me if you make a deal on the sly."

James was too startled to hear this news from a stranger to respond to her hint.

"Where are they moving to?" Maralys asked, untroubled as to where she learned more.

"I hear they're looking at farms."

Farms? James met Maralys' gaze and saw that she was less surprised than he was.

"It must be about the heritage seeds," she whispered and James nodded. He couldn't imagine moving to a farm, let alone all the work it would entail.

But then Phil had founded and later sold a successful landscaping business. He was curious to find out more. Dinah came back as Maralys finished her coffee, and shut up her laptop. "Shall I drive?" she said brightly, and they fastened their coats to leave the diner.

Annette charged into the kitchen at Grey Gables, flushed and flustered. There had been epic traffic coming out of Boston and snow on the roads. The drive had taken twice as long as she'd expected. She'd dropped her backpack in the foyer, yelled hello to her dad, then come to the kitchen where she knew Beverly would be. One end of the kitchen was barricaded off and her grandmother was sitting on a low stool, leaning over three puppies with curly gold fur.

They were adorable, but Annette wouldn't be diverted from her quest.

Beverly spared her a glance, the older woman's gaze sweeping over Annette as it always did. She nodded slightly in approval, then turned her attention back to the puppies. "I like that one," she said, referring to the new T-shirt design. Annette was wearing the burgundy version. "The only thing more satisfying than drinking from the skull of your enemies is feasting upon their livers while still warm."

"I knew you'd understand." It wasn't too hard to recall that Annette had once thought her grandmother was a wicked witch.

They'd come a long way since then, but mostly because of the Jag.

Which was being sold.

In Annette's mind, that travesty took them back to square one.

Beverly smiled a little. "How's the business going?"

"Pretty well, really. That's not what I want to talk about."

Beverly straightened. "I do respect your inclination to get right to the point, Annette."

"You should. I learned it from you."

Beverly stood up then, and the puppies began to circle. "Oh! It's time. Pass me that leash and open the door please."

"You need your coat. It's cold."

Beverly paused and gave her a cool glance. "Unusual concern for my welfare has been duly noted. What *do* you want?"

Annette saw no reason to be coy. She and Beverly had always been blunt with each other. "The car. *My* car."

"It's not your car. It's my car, which means I can do whatever I want with it." Beverly opened the back door, admitting a cold breeze. "And what I want to do is sell it."

"Why? I love that car!"

"It needs too much attention. It's at the point in its life that it should be owned by a mechanic, and I've found the perfect one."

"You could sell it to me."

Beverly glanced back. "What would you do with it? You need that little van for your deliveries. Why would you need two cars? Where would you park it?" She leaned back in the door. "How would you pay for it? How would you pay for fixing it?" She shook her head. "Don't be silly, Annette. It would be a foolish obligation for you."

Annette sat down hard at the kitchen table. "But I love it."

"So do I," Beverly agreed, bringing the three puppies back inside. She gave each one a cookie and a pat, told them all how clever they were, then put them back behind the barricade. One chased a ball and the others raced after it. Beverly sat down opposite Annette. "I thought about giving it to you," she admitted. "I know you love it. But that gets complicated, because I'd have to be fair."

"One Jag, nine grandchildren," Annette said with a sigh.

"Exactly. If you had an inclination to automobile repair, or a boyfriend who had that talent, it would be one thing."

"But then, you should probably give it to Michael. He's mechanically minded."

Beverly shuddered. "He's not even got his license yet, which means he hasn't had his first accident thus has no idea that he isn't immortal. I wouldn't give him a car for at least another decade, and by then, he can buy his own."

"Tough love," Annette said with a smile. "JD would love it."

"Until he had to spend money on it," Beverly noted. "And Jonathan would forget all about it because he got absorbed in an interesting problem."

"True."

"I'm sorry, Annette. I knew you would take it badly but I don't think there's another good solution." Beverly smiled then and her eyes sparkled a bit. "But you know, the young man who has expressed an interest in buying the Jag is very good-looking."

"Wait a minute. Are you fixing me up?"

"Of course not," Beverly said, though she averted her gaze. "But I'm a little too busy to drive the car down there for him to look at it again. I said I'd come by on the twenty-seventh, at two in the afternoon." She met Annette's gaze steadily. "Any chance you could take care of that for me?"

"Beverly!"

"Grandma," Beverly corrected. "And I'd like to be a great grandmother soon, thank you very much."

"You think I'm going to have a guy's kid because you're selling him your car."

"I think you don't appear to be meeting many young men, and that you have a common interest with this one already. How bad can it be to take the car down there and see what happens?"

Annette drummed her fingers on the table. It had to be better than meeting a guy at the gym, while she was a sweaty mess. "All right. I'll do it."

"Good. Thank you." Beverly went to her purse and withdrew a business card, then handed it to Annette. "His name is Scott Sexton. A very nice young man."

Scott Sexton?

It couldn't be the same Scott Sexton, could it?

Even the possibility of meeting the guy she'd idolized in high school made Annette's palms go damp. She took the card and stared at it, a lump in her throat.

Scott Sexton, Thursday at two.

And she'd be driving the Jag.

"Sweet," she whispered under her breath and Beverly smiled.

Maybe she really was the wicked queen, making dreams come true.

Maybe there was a catch.

CHAPTER FOUR

It was starting to snow by the time Zach drove back into Rosemount late in the afternoon on Christmas Eve. He'd been tense all the way back from Boston, because Jen had a doctor's appointment earlier in the day. He always dreaded the results but hoped for the best, and so far, that had worked out well. She'd been cancer-free for thirteen years, but Zach knew he'd never stop treating every day together as a blessing.

He'd definitely become the luckiest guy in the world the day that Jen had agreed to marry him, and he would do whatever was necessary to defend that. Who would have guessed that he'd build a successful career as a photographer? It had started with that one gallery show, the one Jen had goaded him into pursuing. Now he did an annual show of art photographs, sold photographic stock from his website and did family portraits.

Jen had built a loyal family for her knitting store, The Black Sheep, and had regular clients who took road trips from Boston, both to shop in the store and attend classes. She'd bought a small warehouse on the edge of town for the online branch of her business, and sold discontinued yarns and colors from her website. She had two part-time employees there who packed orders and shipped them. She featured local knitting designers twice a month in the shop and everything was going really well.

Their own daughters were growing up now, creative and talented in their own right, and often helped out with one business or the other. Zach would never have gotten his website updates done without his nephew Jonathan and daughter Nicole's help.

If anything, Jen worked too much. She loved what she did, but Zach always worried that she was pushing herself too hard.

He deliberately drove down Main Street before going around the block to park in the back of the shop. The town really looked its best when decorated for the holidays, with cedar roping on the front of every store, wreaths on the doors, and the windows decorated for Christmas. There were more twinkling fairy lights than he could shake a stick at, and a line of kids waiting to talk to Santa in his hut in front of city hall.

Jen had been a big part of the revitalization of the town and he was so proud of her.

He pulled into the parking spot behind her knitting store, then carried the gift he'd gone to the city to collect up the stairs to their apartment. He kissed his daughters, who were both busy making popcorn chains in the kitchen. As usual, Nicole, the older at eleven was instructing Jasinda, just nine, on the most aesthetically pleasing way to get the job done. As usual, Jasinda was intent on doing the job her way and ignoring her sister. Jasinda was blond and tiny, like a fairy child, while Nicole was tall, dark-haired, and athletic. Zach figured Jasinda should have been giving the instructions as this was a creative task, but he knew better than to say anything. He hung up his coat and kicked off his boots, put the gift on the counter, then grabbed a handful of popcorn. The bowl was enormous and nearly empty but there couldn't have been eight feet of garland.

He had a pretty good idea where the rest of the popcorn had gone, and Roxie wasn't even around anymore to help. He frowned, not wanting to think about losing that big lovable dog even for a minute. He missed her all the time.

"What did you buy?" Jasinda demanded. She was already eying the gift, trying to guess what its contents might be from its shape. "It's big."

"An Easter basket," Zach replied, deadpan. "They were a really good deal, although I wonder if the chocolate bunnies might be past their best-before date."

"You did not!" Nicole replied. Neither of his

daughters were easily fooled by his jokes, which was just fine by Zach. They'd be as ready for the real world as he could make them.

"It's a gift for Mom."

"What about us?" Nicole asked.

"Wait until the tree is decorated tonight, then you'll see." They always decorated the tree on Christmas Eve, since Jen put one up in the shop on the Saturday after Thanksgiving.

"Aunt Cin said we should ask you for a *car*."

"Aunt Cin is more trouble than she has any right to be," Zach said, referring to Jen's older sister. "Besides, you're only eleven. What would you do with a car?"

Nicole nudged Jasinda. "I could drive it. Let me drive yours and I'll show you."

"Perish the thought. I'll savor every minute until you're sixteen."

Nicole threaded some more popcorn. "Wait'll we're sixteen, then we'll ask for a car."

"He'll still say no," Jasinda replied.

"He probably thinks we'll share." Nicole rolled her eyes at that.

Zach was thinking it would go exactly like that, that Nicole would always drive and Jasinda would be happy to daydream in the passenger seat while her sister chauffered her around. "How many miles of popcorn garland are you making?"

"Mom said to make lots. She popped a huge bowl for us after school, then went down to the shop."

"I see maybe eight feet of garland and an empty bowl," Zach noted. "That's hardly miles."

"Well, we're running out of popcorn."

"And where did it go?" Zach tickled Nicole's stomach and she laughed. "I guess you're not going to want dinner."

"Of course we do! It's Chinese food night!" Nicole's enthusiasm was probably affected by the fact that they almost never ate take-out of any kind.

"Natalie said so," Jasinda said. "She said she's bringing Szechuan."

"Excellent," Zach said. "She must be bringing it from Boston."

The girls nodded.

He never would get used to the girls calling their grandmother by her first name, but then between his family and Jen's, they had more than enough quirks to go around and that was a comparatively small one. It had started because everyone in the family had called Jen's grandmother 'Gran' and Natalie had wanted to avoid confusion. Gran had passed a few years before, but the habit had stuck anyway.

"Uncle MB's coming, too," Nicole informed him.

"He brings the best candy."

"Dibs on the Turkish Delight," Zach said, just to set them off. It worked and he threaded some popcorn as they debated the merits of all the confections made by Jen's big brother. "How's your mom?" he asked when there was a lull.

"Busy in the store," Nicole said, bored by the question. "Why?"

"Well, she's had you two home all day, and an appointment, and the store to run. I thought she might be tired."

"That's why you brought her a present," Jasinda guessed, eying it again.

"Something like that. Finish up with the popcorn and I'll go check on her. What time are Natalie and the others coming?"

"Seven, Mom said."

"Then we have work to do to get that tree decorated. Can you get out the ornaments, please?"

The girls abandoned the popcorn and did as he asked, Nicole giving advice on which box to move first and Jasinda doing as she pleased. Zach shook his head and went down the stairs to the shop. There was Christmas music playing and the steady ring of the cash register, a sound that made his heart merry at any time of year. He paused at the bottom of the steps and surveyed The Black Sheep. The walls were lined with shelves and stocked with yarns of all colors and widths. In the middle of the floor in the front half of the shop was a wire Christmas tree, a kind of sculpture made by one of Maralys' friends. It looked stark when first set up but by this point in the season, Zach could hardly see the wire frame for all the pairs of mittens hung upon it. The mittens were donated by customers and would be given to the local food bank tonight, along with the contents of the boxes beneath the tree. Jen always got cartons from the grocery store and covered them in wrapping paper, with their tops folded down inside. People brought in non-perishable donations, plus there was a coffee can on the counter for cash donations. They'd take it all down to the food bank before dinner.

Jen was behind the cash register and though she smiled for the customer who had just paid for her new yarn, Zach thought she looked pensive. His chest tightened, but he tried to hide his concern.

"Hey, gorgeous!" he said and swung off the newel post at the bottom of the stairs. "Come dance with me. This is our tune."

Jen laughed along with the customer, who waved as she left. Jen followed and locked the door, then heaved a sigh. "I think it was the busiest day of the month," she said. "And there's really a lot for the food bank. We might have to make two trips."

"A good problem to have."

"An excellent problem to have," she agreed.

"Come dance with me," Zach said, offering his hand.

Jen smiled and dropped her gaze, then put her hand in his as she came closer.

Zach spun her around, then caught her against his chest. "How is it that you always feel so perfect?"

"Might be a result of you liking me."

"Might be," he agreed, pretending to consider it. He began to waltz, leading her around the mitten-clad tree. "What aren't you telling me?" he murmured and she shook her head.

"I never said anything."

"You didn't have to."

"You have serious radar, Zach Coxwell."

"I love you. That means I pay attention."

"More than anyone else who loves me."

"Maybe I love you more," he suggested, then grinned and dipped her low.

"Well, I guess that's the trouble," Jen said solemnly. There was a twinkle in her eyes, but Zach wasn't sure what was amusing her.

"Why is that a problem?"

"It's not, but it has certain...repercussions." She whispered the last word into his ear, the fan of her breath making him shiver.

It also turned his mind in a predictable direction.

"Nicole and Jasinda," Zach agreed. "But I think they're kind of cute." He dipped her again. "Not as cute as their mom, of course."

"Maybe the next one will be," Jen murmured and Zach almost dropped her. He froze and stared into her eyes, noting that then she really smiled. "I do love surprising you, Zach. I don't think that will ever get old," she said and reached to touch her lips to his. "Ready to be a dad again?" she whispered.

Zach grinned, and swirled her to her feet, then caught her close again. He was well aware that there were two girls at the top of the stairs, intent on eavesdropping. Jen clearly was, as well. "You're kidding me," he whispered.

"I'm not."

"This calls for a foxtrot."

"At least you know how to do it now," she countered and they danced across the floor.

Zach halted suddenly and lifted her off her feet. "Wait." He held her gaze and whispered again. "Are you allowed to dance?"

"I can do whatever I want, as long as it feels good."

"Isn't that how you ended up pregnant again?"

Jen laughed. "Pretty much." When he began to dance again, she grabbed two fistfuls of his sweater—a cabled merino wonder that could stop traffic in knitterly circles—and tugged him to a halt. "Are you pleased?" she whispered. "Really?"

"Truly, utterly and completely," he said without a shred of hesitation. "How could I not be?" He pushed a hand through her hair and dropped his voice to a murmur again. "As long as you're okay."

Jen nodded, her happiness more apparent now that she was reassured. "She said I'll have to take it easier this time, because of my age..."

"You're only forty-three."

She sobered and held his gaze. "It might not work out, Zach. Will you be okay with that?"

"I'm good with whatever we do together. We're a team. We'll do our best but it will be as it will be."

Jen nodded agreement and held tightly to his hand. "I don't think we should tell anyone yet," she continued in an undertone, flicking a glance upward. "Let me get through the first trimester first."

"When's the big day?"

"It should be the middle of July, but she warned me that it could be early."

"Okay. What other changes do we need to make? Should Fiona become full-time in the store?"

"Probably not during the winter." Jen bit her lip. "It tends to be quiet. I might close Sunday, Monday *and* Tuesday until March. The extra day won't make that much difference, and I'll probably need the rest. And the only evening we need to be open is Thursday, for the Stitch and Bitch."

"Sounds like the perfect winter to catch up on your knitting," Zach said.

"We have no baby things," she agreed. "I gave everything away after Jasinda."

"Uh huh. This is all a diabolical plan to add to your yarn stash," he teased.

Jen laughed outright. "No, but it is a plan to add to our family."

"Sounds good to me," he assured her, then kissed her as if no one was looking—even though he knew that wasn't the case.

"You said my name!" Jasinda accused and two pairs of footsteps could be heard on the stairs.

"This has to be about presents," Nicole agreed as the girls jumped into the shop.

"Presents?" Zach said with feigned surprise. "Why should there be presents?"

"It's Christmas!" the girls protested in unison.

"But do we know anyone who's been particularly good this year?" he said, looking around the shop as if he couldn't see anyone. Then he glanced down at

Jen and let his expression turn to delight. "Jen! It just so happens that this big guy in a red suit asked me to make a special delivery for him, to you."

"You didn't," Jen said.

"I didn't. It was Santa, honest and true. I'm just the delivery boy."

"I think I know," Jen said, her pleasure clear in her expression.

"It's true that you've been very very good this year," Zach said and they kissed again, more slowly this time.

"What is it?" Nicole demanded. "We don't know."

"There's only one way to find out," Jasinda said and seized Jen's hand. The two girls practically flew up the stairs to the apartment, Jen giving him a glance as she took her time. Zach lingered behind, taking a moment to turn off the lights before he followed. He knew that Jen would love the antique yarn swift because she'd been the one to find it online and had admired it—she just hadn't liked the price. But Matt had dropped off the check, repaying the family loan for Grey Gables, and it had come at a good time to spread a little festive cheer.

Even better, they were having a baby.

Zach was pretty sure he hadn't forgotten everything he knew about babies, and he was honest enough to admit that he hoped it would be a boy this time.

A baby.

The best part of success was being able to share it.

Matt really enjoyed giving those checks to his siblings. They'd believed in him, all those years before, agreeing to let him buy out their shares in Grey Gables after their father's death. At the time, Matt had been terrified that he wouldn't be able to make good on the loan. It was a lot of money, and he'd just left his job to become a writer. He'd had one book written, no agent, no publishing deal—just the faith of his wife and family.

And it had been more than enough.

His first book had been sold at auction to a big New York publishing house and had been launched with enthusiasm. Matt knew it was a stroke of luck that the movie rights had been optioned, and another that a movie actually had been made. It hadn't been a blockbuster—a thoughtful story about two brothers wasn't likely to do that—but it had been enough of a success to pave the way for six more books and three more movies.

Then digital publishing had come along and he had negotiated for the right to write and publish something different. He'd written a mystery series under a pseudonym, a series that was up to twenty titles and still going strong. It sold really well and had been translated into eight languages. Discussions had just begun about making it into a television series.

Matt had everything he wanted, and he knew it was because James, Zach and Phil had given him the chance to follow his dream.

He'd talked to James about their housing options and suggested they start walking daily together once James and Maralys moved. Matt knew he could use more exercise, too. He also had asked James to help him with the contract on the television deal, knowing that his older brother would enjoy the challenge of learning the legalities of performance rights. Maybe that would lessen the blow of leaving the courtroom.

Zach had stopped by the day before on his way to Boston and Matt had enjoyed seeing his youngest brother's face light up when he opened the envelope with the check inside. No doubt with two girls to send to college soon, the money was welcome.

He had one check left, the one for Phil, his baby sister, and he couldn't wait to present it to her.

This Christmas, for Matt Coxwell, was about the joy of giving.

Christmas Day at Grey Gables was always like something out of a movie to Jen. Everything seemed to be perfect in that house, and no expense was ever spared, at least to her eyes. Lights twinkled and snow fell. Crystal sparkled and wine flowed. Everyone dressed up and the girls had new velvet dresses for the day.

Jen figured it was good for the girls to have the contrast between Zach's affluent family and her own. For Christmas Eve, they'd worn jeans and their ugliest holiday sweaters then shared a feast of take-out Chinese food.

She was, in a way, looking forward to seeing the faces of the Coxwells when they learned that her sister, Cin, had bought everyone goats for Christmas. The goats would actually be delivered to families in Africa, as a source of milk. In her family, everyone had been thrilled to send some joy to those with less to celebrate. She and Zach had had a good laugh after everyone left at the reception such a gift might have in his family.

They parked in the crowded circular driveway.

"Last," Zach said with a shake of his head. "Even though we live in town."

"Not last," Jen said, pointing to Nick and Phil's mini-van, which was just pulling into the drive.

Zach laughed. "The locals arrive last. I love it."

"Have you seen the puppies yet?" Phil called, opening her door once the van was parked.

"Puppies?" Jasinda and Nicole asked in unison.

"Three puppies," Phil said with a smile. "Mom's watching them for Ross. They were rescues, just found on Friday. They're in the kitchen."

"How do you know all this?" Zach demanded as they hugged and kissed.

"I had to lend them baby gates."

They laughed together and exchanged holiday greetings. The four girls ran for the front door, and Jen thought Jasinda and Nicole were even more excited than they had been all day. Michael walked behind them, pretending to be too cool for puppies, but Nick grinned. "He'll be down on his knees with them in five minutes," he predicted. "They're really cute."

"Ross didn't want them getting adopted over the holidays," Phil said, getting a bowl out of the back.

"You watch," Nick said. "He'll be matchmaking today."

They laughed together about that.

Zach lifted the dishes from Jen's hands, leaving her with only her purse to carry into the house. She gave him a look, thinking the others would notice, but he just winked.

If they noticed that he was being extra attentive, they didn't say anything.

In fact, Nick seemed to be particularly attentive to Phil. She wasn't carrying anything either.

Surely there couldn't be two new surprise babies on the way.

Then Phil flushed and fanned her face. "Stupid hot flashes," she muttered as she opened her coat. She smiled at Jen. "Wait for it."

"What did you bring?" Jen asked, changing the subject.

"Gluten-free stuffing and a dessert. Did you bring that nut loaf?"

"I did, and Zach's beet salad."

"Excellent. I love both of them." Phil sighed and shook her head. "Another holiday feast, filled with temptation."

"It's Christmas. The food is part of the celebration."

"Then we should get to wear our sweatpants with the stretchy waistband."

"Or at least bring them so we can change later."

They laughed together. "Those puppies are so cute," Phil said. "I'm halfway tempted."

Nick glanced back. "Because you need something else to do?" he asked and Jen sensed an old joke.

"No, I don't. But they're adorable. Little caramel poodles."

"It must be nice for Beverly to have them over the holidays," Jen said as they walked to the house together.

Phil winced. "I know. She really misses Champagne and Caviar."

Zach sobered then, and Jen knew he was thinking of Roxie. The Bernese mountain dog had been a huge lovable part of their family, but she hesitated to suggest adding a puppy, given her own news. Zach winked at her, clearly thinking the same thing.

Then another car pulled into the driveway. They waved at the station wagon, because it was Ross, and he pulled around to the garage. Matt had opened the front door and the kids had gone inside, but Jen and Zach waited for Ross. He was walking really quickly, as if he wanted to catch up with them, but Jen saw that he was being tugged by a large golden poodle.

"This is Freya," he said as she hauled him to the door. "She hasn't stopped whining since Friday and she won't eat. I thought my tech, Maddie, could use a break."

"The mom of the puppies?" Zach guessed.

"And I think she knows where they are. She went crazy sniffing me when I picked her up." Ross leaned in the door and shouted. "Everyone out of the way to the kitchen. There's a poodle coming through!"

James shouted from down the corridor that the way was clear and Ross unclipped the leash. Freya bolted down the corridor and lunged into the kitchen.

"She's on a mission," Zach said.

"She's beautiful," Jen replied and he glanced at her.

Then they heard a joyous bark and a lot of laughter from the kitchen. They all hurried down the corridor. Everyone was in the kitchen, and one end of the room had been barricaded off, just as Phil had said.

"She jumped right over the baby gate," Maralys said.

"Then she was so excited that she jumped back out," James said.

Freya had evidently jumped back inside the makeshift pen. Her tail was wagging so hard that Jen could hardly even see it and the puppies were gathered around her. She was sniffing them and licking them, and one reached up to suckle. She came back to Ross, leaping over the gate again, and licked his hand before returning to her puppies. Then she laid down on the dog bed there and the little ones piled on top of her, wiggling and wagging.

"Maybe she'll eat now," Beverly said.

Ross nodded. "Maybe." He reached for a box of biscuits and Freya graciously accepted one from him, then ate it delicately. Ross pushed a hand through his hair and smiled, his relief obvious. Beverly came to stand beside him, and Jen noticed that she looked happier than she had in a while.

Since Caviar's death.

There was more activity as dishes were put in the fridge, the contents of the fridge were rearranged, coats were hung up and more greetings were exchanged. Matt was pouring drinks, and Maralys was carrying gifts into the living room, where they'd do the gift exchange after dinner. The kids were already scattering and Jen could smell the turkey cooking.

"What a lot of trouble they are," Beverly said, her voice filled with affection. "But they already know to go to the door when they have something to do. They're so clever." She reached over the barrier and one puppy darted to her, licked her hand, then hurried back to Freya. "Now, they're all happy."

"Has Freya been adopted?" Zach asked Ross

Jen held her breath waiting for the answer.

"No," Ross said. "I didn't even want to consider it before the new year. Now, I don't know. It seems as if she needs to be near her puppies. And she still has to gain some weight back, too."

Freya wagged her tail, her expression so bright that Jen thought she could have been smiling. "We could take her," she suggested, slipping her hand into Zach's. "I'd like to have a dog again, and she could come into the shop when she got used to it."

"But..." Zach murmured, concern in his eyes.

"She won't need to be trained. She already is."

Ross nodded. "She is. My tech said her manners are perfect. The only thing is her weight and her concern about the puppies."

"The girls are old enough to take some responsibility, and they have been begging for another dog."

"The question of her weight looks fixed," Jen said as Beverly gave Freya another biscuit and it rapidly disappeared. "Provided you know where the puppies are going to be."

"Of course, he knows where the puppies are going to be," Beverly said crisply. "He knew that the moment he brought them in the door."

Ross began to smile. A bit of color rose on the back of his neck, as if he'd been caught doing something underhanded, and Jen found herself smiling.

"You had a plan," Beverly said.

"I have many plans," he admitted. "They don't always come to fruition. I'd hoped you'd keep one."

Beverly smiled back at him. "All three or nothing at all. They're sisters and need to be together."

Ross smiled not looking surprised at all. "Deal."

Beverly turned to Jen. "Meet Honey, Amber, and Goldilocks." She pointed a finger at Ross, laughing a little. "You knew that if I agreed to look after them for a week, I'd be lost. It didn't even take that long."

Ross grinned. "Well, now that's settled, maybe my second plan can come together, too."

Beverly wrinkled her nose but her eyes were sparkling. "You're going to take advantage of a weak moment, aren't you? You, wicked man." There was no heat in her words and Jen was pretty sure Beverly liked Ross just the way he was.

"Come on everyone," Ross said. "I need witnesses, in the living room."

"Why not right here?" Beverly asked.

"Because I'm going to drop to one knee on a nice thick carpet," he replied and caught her hand in his. "And if your mom says no to me again," he told Zach. "You can all commiserate with me."

"Again?" Jen echoed.

"Not again," Beverly said, then blushed as she followed Ross to the living room. "Although I shouldn't have told you that. The suspense should be part of it."

Nick was never going to be completely at ease when he went to Grey Gables, especially over the holidays when the house seemed to be a bastion of tradition and wealth. He was always a little intimidated by the house, and when it was decorated for the holidays, just the sight of it conjured up all his teenage insecurities—and his awareness that he'd come from the wrong side of the tracks.

But that was quickly followed by his conviction

that he'd married well.

Not just because Phil came from a family with money, though. She was the one for him, the keeper of his star, and he couldn't imagine being without her. He wished he'd noticed her worries sooner, but now that they'd started to talk about things, they were working as a team again. He'd done some research online after she went to bed, and learned a lot more about menopause, which had given him a plan as to how to help her get through it.

She looked fabulous dressed for Christmas in a little black suit with a red blouse. Her earrings were little jingle bells that Michael had chosen for her when he was all of five, and she wore them every year. She was the best mom, and their kids were awesome—creative and smart and balanced. He credited Phil for that. Her little secretive smile still drove Nick crazy and the smell of her skin drove him to the moon. He was sure that he could make love to her every night and day for the rest of his life, and it would still seem new every time.

He was prepared to test that theory.

She took his hand when they entered the house, just like she always did. The kids ran ahead, having no hesitation about Grey Gables.

Nick had been shocked to learn about James' incident and it had shaken Phil. She led them straight to James and Maralys. "Are you okay?" she asked and James had time to nod before Phil hugged him tightly.

She always wore her heart on her sleeve, and

Nick loved that.

"If you need help with anything, let us know," Nick offered as James shook his hand.

"We're looking at houses in town," Maralys said.

"What do you know about those places built on Campbell's old farm?" James asked.

"Good builder," Nick said. "Friends of ours bought there last year and really like it. The house is finished well. I said to Phil that we should look over there."

"You're moving?" Maralys asked in surprise.

"We stayed at the house for Lucia, but it's too much for us." It sounded so simple when Nick said it out loud, and it was true.

"We have seeds to plant," Phil said with a smile. "I don't suppose you're in the market for a stuffed lynx?" she asked, teasing James. "It might give the right touch to your foyer when you move."

Nick nudged her. "Don't spoil the surprise. I was going to give them the sculptures of the crucified thieves as a housewarming gift."

The dismay in James' expression made them all laugh.

"What are you going to do with everything?" Maralys asked.

"Auction," Nick said. "If there's anything you want, speak up."

"I would love to come and look later this week," Maralys said. "Lucia had some really interesting pieces and we have some mad money now."

"Mad money?" Phil asked.

"Shh," James said. "They still don't know."

Know what?

Nick turned and found Matt behind him, grinning as if he was up to trouble. But it had always been Zach who got up to trouble. Matt was the quiet, straight arrow. Nick glanced at Phil, relieved to see that she appeared to be just as confused.

"Step into my office," Matt said, dropping his voice ominously low.

"Said the spider to the fly," Phil said, echoing Nick's thoughts perfectly.

"That's a parlor," Matt corrected, welcoming them into the library with a sweeping gesture. Nick liked this room a lot since Matt and Leslie had redecorated it. The leather couch looked particularly inviting with a fire blazing on the hearth and a Christmas tree sparkling in the corner. Matt's desk was cleared of everything except an envelope.

Matt handed it to Phil with a flourish.

"What's this?" she asked with suspicion.

"Open it and see." Matt smiled, looking like the cat who had swallowed the canary. Phil took a deep breath, a lifetime with three older brothers making her doubt almost every situation. She opened the envelope and pulled out a Christmas card.

That seemed innocuous enough.

Except for the check that fell out of it.

Nick gasped.

"Mad money," Phil whispered. She turned the card so they could both read the inscription. "I didn't think you'd pay off the whole loan this fast!"

she said to Matt.

"Things have been going really well. I wanted to share."

Phil turned to Nick with shining eyes. "A farm," she whispered.

Nick wasn't sure, not now that he'd seen their finances. "Let's see how things look after we sell the house and its contents."

"What farm?" Matt asked.

"Nick wants to transform the heritage seed collection into a business. He thinks we should buy some land and till the seeds, harvest more, and start a heritage seed catalogue."

"Is that why you're selling the house?" Maralys asked.

Nick shook his head even before Phil could answer. "No, it's time for that, but hopefully, time for this new venture, too. We're going to look at smaller places in town."

"You'll still be stretched thin," Matt said. "How about an investor in that new business?"

"Really?" Phil asked.

"Sure." Matt winked. "We can call it seed capital."

"That would be great!" Phil said and Nick smiled.

"It would be great. Let's see how all of this selling works out, then we'll talk."

"You know where I am," Matt said, and shook Nick's hand.

Phil gave her brother an impulsive hug. "Thanks

for the mad money."

"Thanks for the chance to keep the house in the family."

Then everyone was hugging and Nick was included, much to his own surprise. He felt blessed then by his inclusion in Phil's family and more optimistic about what they could achieve together.

They returned to the foyer to discover that JD had just arrived. Maralys teased him that a woman must be responsible for him being late and he'd flushed so that Nick wondered if it was true. JD had brought his mom, Marcia, and her date, Norm, who seemed like a nice guy. They chatted and caught up a bit on each other's lives, admired the puppies, then Beverly called for everyone to sit down.

Annette and Jonathan were organizing the meal in the kitchen while the older generation took their seats in the dining room. Candles shone on the table, the chandelier sparkled overhead, and as usual, there was silver and crystal lined up at every place. It looked perfect and the room was filled with both conversation and laughter. JD carried in the turkey to a cheer of approval. Jonathan worked his way around the table, pouring wine. Zoë, Nicole, Jasinda, Michael, Krista and Alex carried in hot plates and cold, under Annette's instruction, until it seemed that the table couldn't hold one more dish. Nick sat beside Phil in the sparkling dining room with its long elegant table and held her hand, awed that she'd agreed to be his wife all those years before.

Beverly was laughing, showing off her new engagement ring. The puppies were quiet in the kitchen, probably because they and Freya had fallen asleep after an early dinner. Annette turned down the lights and took her place at the table.

"Uncle Nick gets to make the toast this year," she said, sparing him a smile. He tried to hide his surprise but obviously failed. "Don't decline. You haven't done it before and it's time."

"It certainly is," Beverly said.

Nick started to protest but Phil squeezed his hand. He took a deep breath and stood up with his wine glass. "I raise a glass to all of you. Thank you all for contributing to the bounty of this feast we all share each year. Thank you for your companionship and your laughter, for sharing your challenges and your joys. I'd like to thank God on this day of days for the gift of good health, for the luxury of comfort and warmth, for the joy we find in each other's company. Thank you for all these blessings, and may everyone have continued happiness and success. Here's to the Coxwells. May we all prosper in the year ahead."

"Amen," the others said in unison, then glasses were clinked. There was laughter again. Napkins were shaken out and dishes were passed, then Nick saw a flash of gold as Freya left her puppies to slip beneath the table. He saw Jen peek at her and slip a hand beneath the table, but pretended he didn't notice that.

"I don't know how your year could be anything

but fabulous, Nick," Zach said as he passed a salad. He had that wicked glint in his eye that Nick knew better than to trust.

"Don't tell me you drew my name in the gift exchange." Nick felt an old dread rising. Zach was too cocky for this to go well.

"I did. And you're going to *love* what I got you."

"Oh no," Phil whispered, echoing Nick's thoughts.

Nick watched Zach warily, his imagination running wild. "Any hints?"

"It's bigger than Freya but fits in an envelope."

Nick was mystified, but Jen started to laugh. "You didn't?" she whispered to Zach.

"I did. Everyone needs a goat." He gave Nick an innocent glance as Jen started to laugh. "We've all got one, after last night. I didn't want you to feel left out."

"You bought it since last night?" Jen asked.

"Online shopping," Zach confided. "The single best way to acquire goats."

James shook his head and chuckled as he took some salad. Matt grinned, then passed the potatoes.

"How does a goat fit in an envelope?" Nick asked.

"Because you don't really get the goat," Jasinda said. "It's given to a family in your name. You get a card and they get the goat."

"I thought about chickens," Zach confided as he helped himself to potatoes. "But if you're going to buy a farm, you probably actually want to get the chickens, so they can peck around the garden and eat bugs.”

“Natural pest control,” Phil said.

“Exactly,” Zach agreed. “Plus I thought they’d make a mess in the house if they were running around here today.” He frowned and asked his question of the room in general. “Can chickens be house trained?”

“Let’s not find out,” Beverly interjected from the other end of the table.

“So, I promise to buy you chickens if you buy a farm.”

“You probably want some eggs,” Nick teased and Zach laughed.

“Actually, that’s a really good plan. Deal!” They all laughed together, then the meal began.

Beverly was amazed. She sat in the living room beside the fire, Freya on the couch beside her and Honey in her lap. Ross was sitting on her other side with Amber and Annette was rolling a ball across the floor for Goldilocks. Amber watched the ball avidly, then jumped down to join the game. Beverly set Honey on the floor, because she wasn’t as good of a jumper as her sisters, and she trotted toward the ball, too.

“They’re adorable,” Annette said.

“They are,” Beverly agreed. She smiled at Ross. “The very best Christmas gift ever.”

“Nuh uh,” he said, waving a finger at her. “Pets shouldn’t be Christmas gifts.”

"They made Christmas special in the best possible way," she corrected and he smiled.

Then he sighed with mock forbearance. "Here I thought I'd done that myself."

"You brought the dogs," Annette noted.

"And the ring," Ross said.

"Oh, right. The rock." Annette smiled. "It's nice, too."

"It's perfect," Beverly said, holding it up to admire it. The sapphire was square-cut and surrounded by diamonds, an arrangement she found very appealing.

"You probably have six more just like it, but with bigger stones," Ross said. "Do you have any idea how hard it is to buy jewelry for you?"

"No, because you did it perfectly," she replied and smiled at him.

"I've had a bit of time to learn what you like."

They kissed and Annette cleared her throat. When they didn't stop, she scooped up the puppies and headed for the kitchen. Freya jumped down and followed, clearly intent on keeping her offspring in sight.

"I thought she'd never leave," Beverly whispered.

"You wicked woman," Ross whispered. "I think you have a nefarious scheme."

Beverly laughed a little. "What's nefarious about celebrating our engagement?"

"Finally," he teased and stole a kiss. "I was halfway sure you'd turn me down again. Right in front of everyone.”

"Bold play, then.”

“Throwing myself at your mercy was my back-up plan.”

“I don't believe it.” They smiled at each other for a long moment, then Beverly sobered. “I was protecting you that last time.”

“Me or you?” he asked, seeing the truth that had eluded her, just as he always did.

She sighed. “You're right. I was afraid. But we do well together, don't we?”

“I think we understand each other.”

They stared into the fire together, his arm slung over her shoulders, and Beverly felt a wonderful sense of contentment. “Thank you for the puppies,” she said finally. “It's the same thing, really. I would never have brought them here.”

“Because you were afraid of having your heart broken again.”

Beverly nodded. “Exactly the same thing. Thank you.”

“I think hearts need to be tested a little,” he said. “Because when they mend, they're stronger.”

“And we can love even harder than before?” Beverly guessed. She nodded. “I like that. It gives the pain a point.”

“If you didn't love anybody or anything, you'd never get hurt.”

“But it wouldn't be much of a life.” She nodded and tightened her grip on his hand. “I'd drink to that, but I think we should do something else instead." Their gazes met, then locked and Beverly felt her blood heat as Ross smiled.

"Something celebratory," he said, his eyes sparkling. "Any ideas?"

"Just one, but it's a good one." Beverly stood up and gave his hand a tug. "Come to bed, Ross, and I'll show you just what you've gotten yourself into."

He stood up and swung her around, leading her to the door. "I thought you'd never ask," he teased and they climbed the stairs laughing together.

Beverly could hear the muted voices of James and Maralys in the library with Matt and Leslie. Annette, Jonathan, JD and Zoë were in the kitchen, laughing at the puppies. Grey Gables was filled with love and joy and family. Beverly Coxwell realized that against her earlier expectations, on this Christmas night, she was feeling very festive indeed.

∽

THE COXWELLS

Look for more from the next generation of the Coxwells. Annette, JD, and Jonathan will have their stories told next.

More Coxwells
Coming Soon!

ABOUT THE AUTHOR

Deborah Cooke sold her first book in 1992, a medieval romance called published under her pseudonym Claire Delacroix. Since then, she has published over seventy novels in a wide variety of sub-genres, including historical romance, contemporary romance, and paranormal romance. She has published under the names Claire Delacroix, Claire Cross, and Deborah Cooke. **The Beauty**, part of her successful Bride Quest series of historical romances, was her first title to land on the *New York Times* List of Bestselling Books. Her books routinely appear on other bestseller lists and have won numerous awards. In 2009, she was the writer-in-residence at the Toronto Public Library, the first time the library has hosted a residency focused on the romance genre. In 2012, she was honored to receive the Romance Writers of America's Mentor of the Year Award.

Currently, she writes paranormal romances and contemporary romances as Deborah Cooke. She also writes historical romances as Claire Delacroix. Deborah lives in Canada with her husband and family, as well as far too many unfinished knitting projects.

To learn more about her books, visit her websites:
http://deborahcooke.com
http://delacroix.net

www.ingramcontent.com/pod-product-compliance
Lightning Source LLC
Chambersburg PA
CBHW021739190726
48288CB00009B/3107